How does sexuality evolve among lesbians and gay men? What is the underlying nature of homosexual attitudes toward aging? Is censorship ever appropriate? Homosexuals telling their parents—when and how?

Jane Rule's frank opinions on these issues and many other realities and fallacies of homosexual life may sometimes shock. They will also challenge you to reexamine your relationships, your sexuality, your attitudes toward fidelity and commitment—many of your most basic concepts.

In this forceful collection which ranges over life and art and morality, a great writer shares with us her life and the growth and development of her art, and brings her luminous intellect to bear on our own lives.

A
HOT-EYED
MODERATE

JANE RULE

THE NAIAD PRESS INC.
1985

ACKNOWLEDGMENTS

Many of these essays first appeared in *The Body Politic*. Some have been published in *Canadian Literature, Event, Branching Out, Room of One's Own, Radical Reviewer, Resources for Feminist Research, Vanguard, Vancouver Calendar Magazine, Utne Reader* and *West Coast Review*. A few are published here for the first time.

Printed in the United States of America
First Edition

Cover design by Susannah L. Kelly
Typesetting by Sandi Stancil

Library of Congress Cataloging in Publication Data

Rule, Jane.
    A hot-eyed moderate.

    I. Title.
PR9199.3.R78H6 1985   814'.54   84-22831
ISBN 0-930044-57-6
ISBN 0-930044-59-2

FOR HELEN

WORKS BY JANE RULE

1964   *Desert of the Heart**

1970   *This Is Not for You**

1971   *Against the Season**

1975   *Lesbian Images*

1975   *Theme for Diverse Instruments*

1977   *The Young in One Another's Arms**

1980   *Contract with the World**

1981   *Outlander**

1985   *A Hot-Eyed Moderate**

1985   *Inland Passage and Other Stories**

*Available from The Naiad Press.

CONTENTS

PART I: ON WRITING

The Practice of Writing 3
The Canadian Climate 8
Before and After *Sexual Politics* 16
Seventh Waves 21
Inside the Easter Egg 26
Notes on Autobiography 31
Morality in Literature 37
Lesbian and Writer 42
For "Writer/Publisher Relationships: Feminist and
   Traditional" 47
For the Critic of What Isn't There 54
Staking Out the Territory 57

PART II: WRITING FOR THE GAY PRESS

Why I Write for *The Body Politic* 63
Extended Care 66
Hindsight 71

Free To Live 74
Walking Canes 77
The Last To Know 80
Border Crossings 83
The Socially Handicapped 87
The Myth of Genital Jealousy 90
The Question of Children 93
Integration 96
Drag 99
Asking for the Moon 102
Home and Mother 106
Lesbian Leadership 109
The Affirmative Action Novel 113
Straights, Come Out 116
An Act of God 120
Censorship 124
Sexual Infancy 130
On a Moral Educaton 136
Rule Making 143

PART III: PROFILES AND RECOLLECTIONS

This Gathering 153
Judith Lodge, A Profile 156
Takao Tanabe 164
Preview 171
John Korner 174
Elisabeth Hopkins 181
A Profile 186
The 4th of July, 1954 198
"Silly Like Us," A Recollection 205

PART IV: REFLECTIONS

The Cutting of Pages 217
Funny People 224

Ashes, Ashes 228
You Cannot Judge a Pumpkin's Happiness by the
    Smile Upon Its Face 236
The Harvest, the Kill 239

PART I:

ON WRITING

The Practice of Writing

Those questions about creative process which deal with the mechanics of writing have always bored me. Whether I use a pencil, pen, or typewriter is not determined by what is objectively effective but by left-handedness, a bad back, lack of funds, and anyway, who really cares? A far more interesting mechanical question than how each of us gets words onto the page might be why so many writers refuse to drive cars, but that investigation would lead away from the point, which is what aspects of the creative process might be usefully shared with other people.

Two of the most important problems for any writer are locating material and conceiving form. As a very young writer my passion for form served my need to learn the rudiments of my craft and also distracted me from what I felt—wrongly it now seems to me—was my lack of experience. What I really lacked was simply enough distance from my experience to know how to use it. Instead I invented material of a sort that can still make me blush. I wrote about ironically wise talking Minah birds who broke up marriages, black men with yellow hair and green eyes who raped sheep.

3

(After that particular story was read aloud to a writing class, my fellow students burst into "We are little black sheep who have gone astray" every time they saw me.) The only way I can explain those choices is to suppose I was grafting my new sexual edginess onto such reading as *Lassie, Come Home* and *Black Beauty*. At sixteen I simply had no taste. But my appetite for every literary device, every theory of language was enormous. Questions about point of view, symbolism and time occupied me at my desk and away from it. The more complex the form of anything, the more I admired it whether in my own work or in Faulkner's, Joyce's or Virginia Woolf's. In fact, philosophy and aesthetics were more interesting than fiction because principles could be isolated, the human clutter evident in even the purest fiction done away with. There are very young writers who come to their own material guilelessly and learn their craft by simply serving more and more accurately what they have to say. Many more of us, influenced by the academy or not, practice ablative absolutes, archaic synonyms, periodic sentences, points of view entirely beyond us, symbolic structures to rival Dante before we make any attempt to come to terms with what is ours to say. In what can sometimes seem a discouragingly pretentious process, technique is learned.

Writing is, more than is often acknowledged, a craft that has to be practiced, like tennis or the flute. Just as an athlete or musician works long hours in solitary repetition of the hardest techniques of the craft before performing them in game or concert, so a writer needs to concentrate, particularly at first, on what is most difficult. The skill is so complex that a great many of its requirements must become, through dogged repetition, nearly automatic. Otherwise writing a novel would be impossible. In much the same way that any speaker of the language knows how to make subject and verb agree without thinking about it, a writer must develop higher and higher automatic skills so that a choice of sentence structure is rarely mistaken even the first time, so that the dozens of minor technical choices involved in each scene can be made almost without thought. The questions for the beginning writer are often ones too mundane for any teacher of literature ever to raise: how do I stop my characters talking and get into the narrative voice again? How do I get through three months in a paragraph? How do I find words for a sexual experience which will illuminate rather than offend? How do I stop this skateboard of a story going down hill except by crashing into a light pole? These are questions answered not by fine theories but by practice, by being there over and over again until the solution occurs as simply as the familiar way home.

Because we all use language every day, there is an illusion that anyone with adequate intelligence and something to say ought to be able to sit down and write a book about it. But speakers of the language do not practice language as a writer must in order to be prepared to solve the problems that arise. That is why even a second-rate writer can, disappointingly, write a more engaging book than someone with a great deal more to say. That is also why a writer deprived of time to practice the craft continually will rarely emerge as a major voice late in life. We are not as bound to childhood opportunity as ballet dancers, nor as limited by our bodies as any of the performing artists, but we still share with all of them the need to be *practicing* artists. The creative process in any art takes time.

Time is, however, not enough. No matter how many hours of the day, years of a life, one practices language, there is still the question of what to write about. Though books can be a source of all kinds of technical help, they are rarely a place for discovering subject matter or insight. Those who find their subject matter early are usually autobiographical writers. Both the inventors of fantasy and the realists for whom social, political and moral questions are paramount may take longer. Whatever the choice, a certain detachment, aesthetic distance is necessary. Without it, the courage and ruthlessness of the autobiographical writer can become nothing more than vengeful self-indulgence. The clever inventions of fantasy must serve a deeper insight or be found empty tricks. The social realist can turn shallow propagandist. No matter is safe from mean use. None is beneath wonder. All choices are personal and justified only after they have been proven.

As a writer, I have discovered my subject matter in the world we share in common, that is, what we all may experience as distinct from what I experience either in my unique life (autobiography) or my unique imagination (fantasy), though there are certainly elements of both in my work. When I present a character, I neither take a real person I know nor invent a being out of an ideal concept; rather I take half a dozen people I've known who similarly have faced circumstances I want to write about—the loss of a parent, rivalry among siblings, political defeat—and draw even more widely than that on physical attributes, inheritance, social circumstances to make up the character I need for the experience I have designed. If that character slips easily into the slot I have made, I am suspicious, wonder if I have been superficial or glib. A character should, like a real human being, resist categorizing, resist simple-minded solutions. The characters I trust I have usually the hardest time with, for they are often conceived in enough complexity to foil my less interesting plots. I have fairly often written about characters I don't much like but never about characters I don't care about. A subjective quirk of mine is to give each of my characters something of my own. It may be a habit or fear, a cough or a favorite word, an old jacket or a childhood landscape. Whatever it is, however small, it is a kind of talisman against any petty or vindictive treatment. I don't like killing characters even when the structure of a story obviously requires it. I refuse to belittle them.

A circumstance and its resolution are harder for me to come upon than characters to inhabit the experience. Plot often seems to me over-judgmental. It caters to the righteous indignation in us to see characters punished by fate if not by law. I am more interested in insight than in judgment;

therefore, I tend to work on circumstances with modest resolutions, which must not be as morally or psychologically simple as they might seem at first glance. I write a fiction of reversed or at least reserved judgment. More and more I have found myself working with novels because I am interested in writing about groups of people and need that much room. The long tradition of fiction with a central character around whom all others must find their secondary place supports hierarchies I don't find interesting, promotes an egotism that is positively boring. Though it is a common enough fantasy, it is simply not true that any one of us is center of the world. Why should novels perpetuate a false view? In choosing the world we share as my subject matter, my authenticity is more exposed and my compassion more required than either would be in autobiography or fantasy. Those are safeguards important to me as a writer.

Where I live seems to me a question like how I get words on paper, not really relevant to the question of creative process. We live as we can, hoping for that balance of nourishment and peace which will sustain us in our work. I live where I can be sure I am free to practice writing rather than being a writer.

The Canadian Climate

Because I was born and raised in the United States and came to Canada for the first time when I was twenty-five and have now lived over half my life here, I should feel more self-consciously Canadian than a native of the country, more defensively Canadian, if you like. I have written a defense for *The Globe and Mail* called, "Canadian Enough" having to do with what I see as my right to be known as a Canadian writer. What really distinguishes me from native writers is my lack of defensiveness about Canada.

I was not raised to think that anything Canadian is second-rate. I was, like most Americans, entirely ignorant of Canada. My geographic insight was limited to the certain knowledge that I lived in the greatest country on earth. Living in England and travelling in Europe shortly after the Second World War, I discovered large numbers of people who did not feel simple gratitude for America's having won the war and having provided the Marshall plan for Europe's recovery. Nor were people generally convinced that the threat of world communism justified the purges McCarthy was initiating in the United States. I was asked a number

8

of embarrassing cultural as well as political questions about the rights of native Indians and blacks, about the incarceration of Japanese Americans during the war.

When I returned to my own country, I didn't any longer feel at home there. The patriotism which required citizens to be proudly, blindly loyal seemed a peculiar American vice which I no longer shared. In England, though I had not been particularly welcomed as an American, I had been encouraged as a young writer, met with others like me to discuss work, talked with published writers who offered introductions to their publishers. In the States I was, because I hadn't published, dealt with as someone deluded, shut out of the jealously guarded, narrow professionalism of publishing. At the Stanford Writing School, where I expected to meet others like me, I found instead a focus on commercialism and negative competition. We were not being groomed for the long apprenticeship required of a writer but expected to emerge out of the head of Zeus, with best sellers as noisy as the atom bomb.

After teaching on the east coast for two years and saving enough money to take a year off for my own writing, I returned to California to visit my family and incidentally took a trip north with a cousin who had never seen the redwoods. We drove as far as Vancouver only because an English friend of mine had been hired at UBC, and I thought I might scout out an apartment for him.

We arrived on a clear August day in 1956, and there before us was a city of human scale (the only two highrises were B.C. Hydro and the Vancouver Hotel) defined by thirty miles of accessible beaches and the mountains of the north shore rising abruptly into forest wilderness. As we drove along the tree-lined streets, seeing gardens as loved as English gardens, then out through the grant lands to a university on cliffs overlooking the sea, I kept wondering why nobody had ever told me of this place, so rarely beautiful, on a coast I'd known all my life. Until that day, that coast had ended for me at Seattle.

It was a good time in the city's history for its aspiring young. The university was expanding by thousands each year. The CBC was in a period of regional assertiveness. The first really professional selling gallery, The New Design, had just been established. From the beginning of my life in Vancouver there was work to do, marking papers and tutoring students for the UBC English department, reading tv scripts for CBC, free-lance broadcasting. When I again needed a full-time job, I was Assistant Director of International House the year the new building was opened. Then I taught in the English department, for, though I had only an honors BA in English and a casual year's graduate work in England, the university needed more teachers than they could find for the hugely expanding enrollment. The four-month-long summer holidays gave me free time to get on with writing.

In those early years the McConnells hosted a writers' group where I met Bob Harlow, Phyllis Webb, and Maria Fiamengo. Bob Patchell, a producer for CBC, was also a member of that group and bought a story of mine he'd heard there for *Anthology*. The McConnells founded their own publishing house, Klanak Press, and brought out an anthology of our short stories, *Klanak Islands*.

A group of artists of all sorts gathered to form The Arts Club. I was on its first board of directors with Geof Massey, architect, Tak Tanabe, painter, Alvin Balkind, director of New Design Gallery. When we rented a building in downtown Vancouver, even Lawren Harris, one of the Group of Seven painters, came down to help clean it up and redecorate it with us. Nearly all the painters belonged, John Korner, Jack Shadbolt, Gordon Smith. Arthur Erickson was a member and gave a wonderful lecture on the process of designing his legendary Comox house. The writers gave readings. I first heard Dorothy Livesay's poetry there. In the early days we didn't have the money which was later available to turn the Arts Club into a theatre club as well, but it gave us all a meeting place, provided us with a community of friends as well as an audience.

Though I published very little in my first half dozen years in Vancouver, I felt supported by that community of artists. The university provided me with a living, but no university is a very good climate for a young writer since academics need to distinguish between "literature," so worthy of their devotion, and "creative writing," practiced by dabblers without PhDs or by themselves in semisecret. Among other artists, my calling was considered neither silly nor pretentious but the hard, long, lonely work it was. We celebrated when any one of us had a show, a performance, a building, something published. And a remarkable number of us survived to take our places not only on the local and national scenes but to international accomplishments and recognition, far more than any people I had known in the States or England.

So for me Vancouver was a remarkably rich and nourishing place, and increasingly I felt I belonged there. More gradually I began to have a sense of British Columbia. As a university chaperone, I toured the province with the Players' Club, presenting Tennessee Williams' *Glass Menagerie* to places as isolated as Bralorne, the gold mining town, as far north as Smithers and Prince George, all through the Okanagan. We were billeted and entertained by local people. Still populated by immigrants, it was a west much younger than the western United States. In British Columbia a dozen cultures mingled uncertainly in towns, in small towns isolated by great reaches of wilderness, mountains, deserts, lakes and rivers, and I felt the more a part of it because I was an immigrant, too.

It took longer for me to have a sense of Canada as a country. When I traveled, I went either south to see my family and friends or to Europe which went on offering me insights into art, history, my own experience. My first published novel, *Desert of the Heart*, was first accepted by MacMillan of Canada. In the early 60s it was still nearly unheard of for a novel to be published in Canada alone. Mine was accepted on the condition that I find either an

American or English publisher to share the costs. Since the book was set in Nevada, it seemed sensible to look for an American publisher. Nearly two years later, when it had been rejected by twenty American firms, I took the manuscript to England where it was accepted by Secker and Warberg, the first publisher to see it. When the book came out and was reviewed across Canada as well as England, I felt welcomed by the country as I had not been by my own, which took yet another year to publish the book to a silence so familiar to first novels there.

If I hadn't been living in Canada, my long apprenticeship might never have come to an end. Yet the native Canadian writers all around me were more often bitter at the lack of opportunity in Canada, the necessity of commanding a market either in England or the States before they could be heard here. They felt cut off from the rich markets to the south, claiming that American publishers weren't interested in Canadian material. My own experience made me think that American publishers weren't interested in American material either but only in success; for, once I'd been published in England and Canada, American magazine editors began to accept my work. They didn't seem to me prejudiced against Canadian settings, only against unknown writers.

Redbook once asked me to name the city a thousand miles from Seattle from which one of my characters was driving and suggested Winnipeg. Winnipeg? The city a thousand miles away from Seattle is San Francisco, but Redbook thought of me as Canadian and therefore chose Winnipeg. After my initial surprise, I happily concurred.

When I exchanged my envied and disliked American citizenship for Canadian, I did not take on the defensive bitterness that seemed to be a Canadian birthright. At first I felt modestly guilty when I traveled in Europe, enjoying a friendly welcome I hadn't received as an ugly American. Though living in Canada had changed me, had given me a sense of citizenship I'd never felt in the States, I knew that

I had not really become someone else. It helped me to remember that one set of my great grandparents had gone from Nova Scotia to northern California to settle. I was named for that great grandmother. I had personal roots to claim in Canada.

I had never applied for an American grant. Educated in the west, I had a notion that without any connection with the eastern establishment, I had no chance of success. I had to apply four times for a Canada Council grant before I was given one, but it was extended for another remarkable year during which I could continue to confirm myself as a professional writer and serve my craft with the intensity of attention that is essential for its maturing.

I have since served on juries for Canada Council. Though women and westerners are not fairly represented either on juries or as successful candidates, it is a quite remarkably good system for supporting artists in Canada. Canada Council is not a patriarchal charity as some of the big American foundations seem to me. It is an organization susceptible to change and improvement.

The Writers' Union of Canada is another institution envied by Americans who are just now trying to organize their own. It's very unlikely that any agent of their government will be willing, as the Canada Council is, to pay the travel expenses of every member of the Writers' Union to attend annual general meetings in or near Toronto or Ottawa. As a result of being able to meet once a year, members from the most remote regions of the country have an opportunity to be active members and don't feel that the organization is really for the benefit of the eastern establishment only. Also it gives them a yearly opportunity to call on their own publishers, on book stores. Though most of us care about our increasing lobbying force on issues like copyright laws, payment for public use of books in libraries, and rely on the Union to help us with contract disputes with publishers, to organize reading tours, it is our sense of professional community which is most important to us.

Publishing, like all other business, is suffering hard times. For perhaps ten years, aided by substantial grants from the government, publishers were able to accept Canadian books for the Canadian market without having to seek publishers in either England or the States. Now again Canadian writers are having to find other markets for their books to be published in Canada at all. My last two books have not had a Canadian publisher because the only one interested wanted international rights without having the staff to handle the distribution problems of that larger market. I have also had to go to the States to find publishers willing to reprint my books and keep them in print for the growing academic market for them, both in Canada and the United States.

Canadian publishers haven't yet taken full advantage of the remarkable changes taking place both in Canadian schools and universities which now for the first time are offering a variety of courses in Canadian literature. Imitating the establishment publishers in the States, they are trying to sell books like cottage cheese, the hardbacks stamped, "Best read within six months," the paperbacks, "Good for six weeks," thereby losing the entire academic market, for the books are out of print before there is time to put them on reading lists, and it often takes years before they are reprinted. We have too few small presses staffed well enough to serve their own back lists as well as they should. In the States, where small presses have to depend on sales rather than grants to survive, both writers and readers are presently better served.

Nevertheless, my American reprints are noticed in the Canadian media. Though too few books written by Canadians are reviewed in newspapers and magazines, we have better radio coverage than any American writer can hope for. Though we don't have much tv coverage for selling books, CBC is commissioning scripts for both radio and tv adaptation of stories and novels. The extra income as well as the increased audience has helped a number of us to stay at our desks.

Very few artists in any country ever make a handsome living, and even fewer of those who do make a lasting contribution to their cultures. Canada, with all its real limitations, most severe of which is its inferiority complex, is a remarkably good place to begin a writing career. It also has a greater opportunity than many other countries to distinguish between those books which are something like cottage cheese and those which are important as part of our heritage. Canada is still able to design institutions on a human scale. We are increasingly supportive of our gifted young. We are growing in our awareness of the strength of our own literature. Courses in Canadian literature are now being offered in universities all over the world.

Most writers are defensive about any label that has a potential for limiting their audience, whether it is "woman," "black," "academic," "regional," "popular," or "lesbian." Unlike some writers, I like the label "Canadian." I chose it, feel at home with it, and know it travels very well in the world.

Before and After *Sexual Politics*

I look back on my formal education, which ended in 1953, and most of my own teaching, which ended in 1973 except for an occasional writing seminar, with an increasing sense of its unreality. Oh, I learned and I hope I taught skills that are useful, aesthetic standards which still measure my own work. What I didn't learn and rarely, until the last couple of years, taught was an evaluation of content.

To be concerned about content was a grave error in critical judgment revealing a subjective and uncultured mind. Moral and political interpretations of literature were invasions of the writer's psyche by upstarts in a dubiously new discipline which should limit itself to the study of rats. Even biographical criticism was suspect because the life more often distorted than illuminated the work. The knowledge that Milton disliked his wife and abused his daughters must not make a reader suspect that his portrait of Eve stemmed from misogyny rather than a clear insight into the nature of woman.

The best way to deal with content was to make it disappear. We were taught, "Form is content," studied therefore only the aesthetics of a work, image patterns, allusions, plot structures, sentence rhythms, devices for telescoping time. If by this method content couldn't be driven entirely away, the history of ideas was brought to bear on it. Perhaps there was anti-semitism in *The Merchant of Venice* (some of my fellow students were survivors of the German camps), but Jews in the 16th Century were money lenders, therefore usurers according to Christian doctrine, and nobody liked them.

I not only didn't object to this instruction, I reveled in it. Even in my teens I identified myself as a writer, and I badly wanted to learn just those skills close analysis of a passage of prose or poetry taught. Since I also already knew I was a lesbian, I certainly didn't want future critics of my work prying into what was then my private life or my psyche to do it. Letting Shakespeare, Milton, and even Dante off those hooks was a small enough price to pay for my own protection.

"Form is content," I preached to my students in my turn. For future writers I still don't think it's a bad place to begin, for there are real critical errors made by imposing alien ideas on a work, requiring from it what it never intended to be. Yet, once the aesthetic whole has been perceived, there is small real value in literature if its content is not considered.

I felt so guilty about my distaste for some great writers that I usually taught them better than I did my own favorites whose strengths seemed so obvious that they didn't need extra selling. I would not have dreamed of telling my students I found Jane Austen a mean-minded prig. I dutifully concerned myself with her sentence structure, plot structure and irony. About George Eliot, whose world was so much larger, richer, and realer to me, I was perfectly willing to admit her failures in plotting, her occasional heavy-handedness. I made no comment at all about her irregular private life or Jane Austen's stifled one.

Long after I had come to terms with my life as a lesbian,

no longer much concerned about protecting my privacy, except in terms of time and space, I went on protecting other writers, both the dead and the living, avoiding as much as I could all the gossip about them. I didn't like to say Gertrude Stein was a lesbian. I didn't offer Virginia Woolf as a suicide. These were irrelevancies. I was so high-minded that I could resist the temptation to tell my students when we came to Auden's poems that I had, the summer before, slept in his pajamas and his bed. (We had lost all our luggage on the way to Austria, and he had given up his bed to us for the single bed in the guest room.) Nor did I tell them I'd asked him no questions about hard places in his poems; it would have been the lowest form of cheating to ask a writer to explain his own work.

I date my awakening to content with the reading of Kate Millett's *Sexual Politics*. Until that time I considered my own likes and dislikes in literature my private taste, to be shared with friends perhaps, but certainly not with students, certainly not in public. By the time I had finished reading that book, furious with the misogyny it revealed, I was not a different private person, but I had come out of the critical closet to know that if moral and political evaluations of literature were important to me as a person, they were important to everyone. Such ideas were far better out in the open where critical prejudices and excesses could be exposed, where values could be tested.

When I had dealt with murder in the third act of a five act Elizabethan play as a structural device of plot, when I had dealt with the mass murders of the fifth act as a convention of the revenge play, when I had discussed the tragic flaw of the hero which would count him among the dead, I hadn't really at all dealt with the moral implications of violence. *Hamlet* for me is partly a great play because Hamlet does concern himsef with conflicting values, never mind whether that makes him the forerunner of the modern hero. I've always cared about moral debate, but I didn't, as a teacher, say so. Such a value judgment seemed to me outside my responsibility as a critic or teacher.

That the *Divine Comedy* is the work of a sadistic mind is not all there is to be said about that great work, but studying it and teaching it without ever raising the issue, which I did, seems to me grossly irresponsible. We may forgive great works all kinds of flaws, but we must not pretend they are not there.

Only in my last year of teaching, which was in the creative writing department at UBC, did I deal not only with the students' prose but with their subject matter. Since I was the only woman in the department and more than half the readers of fiction are women, it seemed to me important to let students know what implications their work had for women, particularly when I was confronted with the rape fantasies of male students.

If I were to teach literature again and had any influence on the selection of material, I would use rather than discount my own taste. I would be urgent in introducing great writers who have been neglected, like Willa Cather and even George Eliot. I would not neglect aesthetics which still seem to me central to the study of literature, but I would include political, psychological, biographical and moral questions where they seemed to me relevant. I would expect my students to take literature as seriously and personally as I do. It would require that I be more vulnerable as a teacher than I have ever been. It would create a whole new range of possible error and distortion for which I used to have easier answers. I may be able to imagine such teaching only because I don't intend to do it again.

I have not ever been primarily a teacher. Writing has always been my first commitment. I've never had any doubt about my own work that the quality as well as the range of my life affects it. My commitment to it has always been moral as well as aesthetic. Form is content only when it means that books are made out of words as a chair is made of wood, not for the wood to disappear but to be made useful.

The power of literature is and always has been its addressing not simply the aesthete but the whole person. It does so because it is written by the whole person of the artist. Yes, we are creatures of our culture as well as individuals. Our failures, like mine as a teacher, can be explained by our own education, but not explained away.

Women's studies courses are suspect not only because the writing of women is often dismissed as second rate but because the material is being treated as seriously as I have suggested it should be. A work of art is not a clever puzzle to be solved by clever readers; it is a passionately articulated vision to be intensely shared. Women everywhere are returning to that reality, buying, reading, studying literature in that spirit. We disturb not only the living but the dead behind whom the living try to hide. George Eliot lived in sin; Willa Cather and Gertrude Stein were lesbians; Virginia Woolf committed suicide (on my birthday, damn her), and so did Sylvia Plath. Let us make no silly myths about any of them but understand their voices out of their personal and cultural histories calling across to us their singular truths to move, test and free us into our own power.

Seventh Waves

Literature and politics have never been easy bedfellows. The one great political work we have, *The Divine Comedy*, was written by Dante in exile against nearly everyone. Though many good and even great writers have revealed strong political biases in their work, they are not remembered long for the way they voted or revolted. Literature is the citadel of the individual spirit which inspires rather than serves the body politic. Those movements which have shunned their writers or required them to follow the party line have got the literature they deserve.

The women's movement in Canada, if it were able to dictate to writers, might have made that mistake, but, except for the gallant small publishers like Daughters, Inc., Moon Books, Naiad Press, Diana Press, Women's Press, all but one in the States, the literature of the movement is published by a press women don't control. If writers are dictated to, it is by what male publishers in New York think women will buy. In nonfiction, women have been served remarkably well with such excellent books as *Sexual Politics*, *Women and Madness*, *Literary Women*,

Beyond God the Father, Of Woman Born, but in what is called literature, the audience has done much less well. I think there is an unhappy conspiracy between women and the establishment press in the States, which has encouraged writers to concentrate on a confessional literature of masochistic defeat. Publishers are convinced that the mass of female readers can and will identify with such books. Writers feel absolved of the accusation that they are leaders, elitists. Writers who began with intellectually adventurous and disciplined works are now anecdotal and personal. Kate Millett who could beard Norman Mailer must redeem herself by showing us that, in real life, she loses her lover to a man. Phyllis Chesler who taught thousands and thousands of women to turn away from psychiatry to health is now selling profiles of the men in her life. Those writers who have been fostered by women's presses are suffering a different but equally deadly limitation of political correctness. Rita Mae Brown, whose *Rubyfruit Jungle* was too didactic but marvelously alive, gives way to a wooden second novel where characters are nothing but political stereotypes: the young radical and the middle-aged career woman. Only in poetry are there women associated with the movement who haven't been reduced by it. Adrienne Rich, who was well established before there was a movement, speaks with a voice which will never neglect intelligence or passion for party line. Her newest book, *The Dream of a Common Language,* does inspire rather than serve the cause.

The literary circumstance in Canada is different. Aside from periodical publications like *Branching Out, Emergency Librarian,* and *A Room of One's Own,* and the one publisher, Women's Press, the women's movement has no press of its own to encourage or require conformity to certain political views. Most of our establishment press are branch plants who take direction from New York or London and tend to be conservative about anything homemade, and even bonafide Canadian publishers like McClelland and Stewart know how to exploit writers only after the fact of their books. The women's movement arrived in Canada at a time when most of the country's respected writers were women, on whom the movement belatedly tried to put its stamp. Margaret Atwood and Alice Munro bridled; Margaret Laurence tried to be polite; Dorothy Livesay, an old hand at politics, took it as one more arrow in her quiver. Gradually nearly everyone agreed that in one way or another the women's movement in Canada had helped women writers by being a newly honoring audience, by making men nervous enough to want to know what women were saying. Canada still does not have writers either created or controlled by the movement.

I want to argue that, no matter how inadvertent this development, it is something we should be profoundly grateful for, much as we are for our abundance of natural resources and small population. For our women writers, not early curbed into narrow didacticism or personal confession, have developed voices which do accurately describe for us the climate in which we live. They are being our historians, sociologists, psychologists. With their testimony we have an opportunity to make more informed political judgments because we have an understanding of our complex and particular culture only a real literature can give.

In a report on her trip to Australia, Margaret Atwood mused on Australia's lack of honor for its Nobel Prize winning writer, Patrick White. When she commented on it to an Australian, he explained, "We cut tall poppies down." It is a mark of colonial mentality to be envious and mistrustful of excellence, to feel exploited and betrayed rather than enlightened by the articulate and intelligent. Canadians less brashly and more sullenly hack away at what is growing tallest in their own landscape, and women, a colonized group within the colony, can be the most frightened and hostile of all, having borne the exploitation of the exploited. That mistrust is an inevitable part of the experience, but it is too often labeled a strength rather than a weakness and allowed to minimize if not destroy the finest specimens blooming in its own soil.

Margaret Atwood is one of our tall poppies. Too many women complain of her success, the number of times she appears on television and radio and on the covers of magazines. Too few take time instead to read *Lady Oracle* as a survival handbook for that wily underdog, woman, who among the pretensions and pressures of the male world secretly leads her own dubious life. Margaret Atwood is not too good for us. She is, like half a hundred others, good enough.

Elizabeth Brewster who is never, to my knowledge, on television or magazine covers, says of herself and other poets, "I think we are being given the same messages." It doesn't matter if the words repeat themselves from poet to poet,

> as long as what is said
> rises like the tide in all our separate waves
> and beats upon and shapes the dreaming shore.

She is our seventh wave, taller and therefore more able to shape that shore but speaking the same messages.

A political movement which defines equality by its lowest common denominator will reject the very power it needs to shape tomorrow. In Canada we have a remarkable number of gifted and articulate women who will not be reduced to what New York or feminist presses think women want to read. They will not be made into political leaders or scapegoats either. They will be our voices if we live up to their intent, severe, humane visions, if we learn to grow with rather than cut down those who have so much to offer us and in our name. It is not a question of whether Margaret Atwood or Elizabeth Brewster are feminists but whether the women's movement is confident enough to claim their power without reducing it to any sort of narrow

political correctness. That confidence is found in much of
what is being written by women in Canada, even for instance
in the small parenthetical statements of Atwood's Susanna
Moody poems:

> (each refuge fails
> us; each danger
> becomes a haven)

or in Brewster's quiet talking to herself about her failure
twenty-four years ago to kill herself:

> . . . you're still here
> And Sylvia Plath isn't.

The poet we have lost, Pat Lowther, didn't kill herself.
She was murdered by her husband. Our politics must have
as one goal an end to that kind of killing. Our collective
voice must grow stronger for the singers in our midst, learning both to deserve and to defend our gifts, our gifted.

Inside the Easter Egg

Inside the Easter Egg, Marian Engel's collection of short stories, was published by Anansi on December 24, 1975, a date not well suited to Christmas sales, and was followed early in 1976 by *Bear*, eclipsing *Inside the Easter Egg*, which should have a more prominent place in the Engel canon than it has yet achieved.

The stories are presented under three headings, "The Married Life," "Ziggy and Company," and "Children and Ancestors," but they all share preoccupations with marriage, with parents and children, with "the sallow shadow of righteousness" cast by religious backgrounds, whether Catholic, Protestant, or Jewish, which the women, particularly, find constricting. The characters also have a habit of turning up in each other's stories. Ziggy is first come upon as the friend of Alex, the main character in "Amaryllis," before he is given a section of his own. Ruth is introduced as Ziggy's first wife in "Home Thoughts from Abroad" and turns up again first on her own in London, then later married to Barney. Marshallene, a writer, not only contributes two pieces of her own, "Marshallene on Rape" and "Marshallene at Work" but is heard on the radio and on the telephone in "Bicycle Story" which belongs to Ruth. The overall impression of *Inside the Easter Egg* is that some of the stories about "all of us" have been told, but a rich vein of human experience remains to be mined.

A novelist chooses to write short stories for all sorts of reasons, some of them too subjective to discover. One of the clues in this collection is Marshallene brooding about a popular book she has written and is unsatisfied with because it should have been made "with many blank pages, pressed flowers and rhymes." A collection of stories can suggest blank pages as well as suggest connections which could be developed: "I could tell you more about my father," Ruth says, "but it isn't necessary." Both deftly shorthanded pasts and a richness of quickly sketched characters allow *inside the Easter Egg* to be the sort of book Marshallene didn't write. Characters in short stories are more like friends you drop in on, whose histories you know only in arbitrary anecdotes and quirky facts, than like the family you live with as you also live with characters in a novel.

Short stories also give a writer freedom to explore themes from many different points of view. Point of view for Marian Engel is of symbolic as well as technical interest. The title story, "Inside the Easter Egg," allows not only the main character, Mary, in hospital to have her tubes tied, an interior thought process, but also her husband, her mother and her oldest daughter. But it is very like stories from one character's point of view, if that character is a woman, because women are preoccupied with how other people feel and what they are thinking. Stories from a male point of view, like "Amaryllis" and "Nationalism," are more decisively limited to what a man wants, how he goes about getting it and what judgments he must make. The men are either frank opportunists, like Ziggy, or have "a core of righteousness," like the husbands who try to stay married. Women, on the other hand, are taught that it is "the highest virtue to see [themselves] as others saw [them]." They always know that, as the title of one story expresses it, "I See Something. It Sees Me." The main character in "Ruth" is aware of being watched and of watching other people "to peel them like grapes and get the skin off them."

Neither manner of dealing with the world is without pitfalls. Men, whether like Alex in "Amaryllis," who is too fastidious to be able to live with the mess of a wife and child he loves, or like Ziggy, whose answer to each of his wives, in turn, when she wants something he does not, is "You're my wife," do not get their way for long. The woman who sees herself as others see her at forty loses her own reflection in the mirror and can only gradually and imperfectly coax it back with "I love you, me."

Men in these stories are apt to be successful in their work. They are anthropologists, philosophers, lawyers, architects, teachers. They tend to be children of parents who push them through the door of education into the middle class where they are glad, grateful and proud to be since they have earned their privilege. For their women, it is a different matter. "She was good at her work, but she married. She would have thought of herself as an awful failure if she hadn't." Those who are good at marriage think, as Mary does about her husband, "If you can't change Osborne, you change yourself," even as radically as being sterilized because he won't be. Alissa, in "The Fall of the House that Jack Built," does not complain when her husband without her permission remodels her grandmother's house for resale rather than living in it because she knows he is restless and needs to be in command not only over her but over what he has perceived as her superior background. Or they offer immediately, as the main character does in "Only God, My Dear," at the moment a husband is tempted to stray, "Do you want me to give up work?" Those who are bad at it say, "Go to hell" to Ziggy, one after another. They don't so easily "get over their backgrounds." They see themselves "playing roles foisted on them generations ago." Or they have affairs, as in "The Salt Mines" and think

"If this is sin, I love it." "It gave her great joy to be finally vulgar." That vulgarity is a combination of sexual abandon and of being with a man who is socially "invisible" because he is a foreigner. Or they drink, in the vacuum of their improved status, their children taken from them for private boarding schools, and finally kill themselves like Isobelle in "Tents for the Gandy Dancers."

In "Bicycle Story," which ends the book, Ruth, because she is listening to Marshallene talk about childhood on the car radio, accidentally knocks her own mother off a bicycle. A large and authoritative woman who has always intimidated Ruth, she is not as badly hurt as Ruth who is bitten by her mother's dog. But the accident gives Ruth a sudden sense of authority over her world. That euphoria comes more from pain killers and whiskey than from the reality of her circumstance as is obvious in the final line, "I opened the window and told the birds they could sing."

Ruth "[is] not religious, reality [keeps] intruding," though religious imagery comes naturally to her. She, for instance, feels lust "darting like the Holy Ghost." It is vital sexuality that is celebrated all through this collection. Ziggy, for all his male chauvinist piggery, "laughs in bed," is as hairy as the gorillas he studies, and, though his women leave him, he can always find another because he likes women and women like him. It is Christian to forgive the sinner, but forgiveness here is pushed dangerously and gladly to the sin as well, for sinning teaches people to free themselves from stultifying righteousness. In "Mina and Clare" Bob has to commit adultery to forgive it in others. The salt mine of the title of that story is not a place of punishment but the magnificent setting for an illicit sexual union. Ruth thinks "I should be guilty. But salt is really not at all like sand," removing the image further from Dante's image of "burning sand" as a punishment for lovers.

When *Inside the Easter Egg* first came out, I was too ill to read it myself. It was read aloud to me, and I was constantly threatened with laughter. Ruth, after she has left

Ziggy, defines living alone as "having no one to tell your one-liners to." Fortunately a writer has the world of readers, and Marian Engel's one-liners are wonderful. "Sublet" begins with "By virtue of the powers vested in me by the Criminal Court of Canada, I now pronounce you man and wife," which weds Ziggy to his third wife. When the daughter in "Meredith and the Lousy Latin Lover" chastises her long absent father for his treatment of her mother, he says, "Tell me what you're doing in school. Women's Studies and what else?" Like one-liners, surprise turns of event are used to fine comic effect. Ceilings fall in, mothers are knocked off bicycles. (Husband Barney remarks about that incident, "That's the trouble with places this size, isn't it? Whoever you knock down is bound to be a relation.") Marian Engel is as funny in sustained description, Ruth in a seafood restaurant in London unable to abide fish, Ruth on the long female hair of her students, to whom she hands out rubber bands for examinations, Ziggy with his gorillas. Hers is not the ridicule of satire. Though each of her characters is sometimes ridiculous, she is not and doesn't intend the reader to feel superior to them. They are much more often to be laughed with than laughed at, for they are all inside those miraculous scenes in the Easter Egg which, truth to tell, are scenes in the real world.

Notes on Autobiography

For some writers there is no choice between fiction and autobiography. Anais Nin, for example, stood in such awe of the novel that her own are often painfully self-conscious and artificial. Only in her diaries, which for years she considered a vice, was she free to express her real perceptions and insights. Violette Leduc, after years of disguising her life in fiction, made her mature works by translating her earlier novels back into autobiography. The value of both these brilliant contributions to autobiographical literature is in the extraordinary candor of personal analysis and confession. Obviously what drew these writers to fiction in the first place was the opportunity to tell personal truth in an acceptable disguise. If that is the only motive, an artistically successful novel is rarely the result; for invention in fiction must serve to make the imagined world truer and more vivid and can only falter when used simply to make the real world less recognizable. Those writers who present frankly autobiographical fiction, like Audrey Thomas, are not trying to protect themselves or the people around them by fictional device. Instead, they are choosing freedom from fact to heighten and clarify their own experience.

The motive for writing autobiography can be as simple as the desire to share interesting experience. Worldly success nourishes most egos enough to inspire, if not autobiography, a careful saving of papers for a future biography. Those whom the world has not given self importance may still feel their lives are of value to grandchildren. The desire to have been of some account is nearly universal, and autobiography can be a way of testifying on one's own behalf, justifying the use of a life. Or, more painfully, it can be a confession, an act of penance. Whatever the motive, understanding and making experience manifest are the talents required.

All writing is craft. A person who sits down at the end of a life in which language has been only a minor tool will almost always write badly. Ghost writers often make a better living under other people's names than under their own, borrowing lives which, practicing their craft, they have not had the opportunity to live. A genuine autobiography is usually written by someone who has devoted a great deal of time to language. Anais Nin began her diary when she was a young girl, wrote it all her life. Violette Leduc's long practice as a novelist prepared her.

Autobiography is not easier than fiction. The dictum even for a fiction writer is "write about what you know." But how many people really know themselves or the people closest to them? So much of assigning motives in life has nothing to do with insight but is rather a dubious moral exercise for the purpose of defending and justifying oneself, finding fault with others. It takes a rare, dispassionate intelligence to see the self from outside, a rare, compassionate intelligence to see others from inside. A willingness to be honest is not enough for those who have lied to themselves for so many years that they have come to believe the images of themselves they have created. Political autobiographies, for instance, rarely avoid campaign promises even long after all the elections have been won and lost.

Because even good memories are faulty, writing something like a continuous autobiography, as Anais Nin did, is the best insurance against losing or falsifying past selves and friends. Only a fraction of what Anais Nin wrote has finally been published, carefully selected and edited in her old age, which provides a critical distance very useful for tempering past excesses of enthusiasm or rage, self love or self pity.

Autobiography of the sort written and immediately published is, by far, the most difficult. One way writers avoid presenting a self so inflated as to block out even the immediate landscape is to take their experience more seriously than they do themselves. James Baldwin in *Notes of a Native Son* and *Nobody Knows My Name* asks his readers to understand that what happens to him happens to black people. His experience is important because it is shared by many others.

Very popular now is the sort of autobiography partly inspired by the women's movement. Kate Millet in both *Flying* and *Sita* writes out of the center of the suffering mire of her life, martyred by the media after the success of *Sexual Politics*, awed by the sudden attention, however negative, she can command. Older values of modesty, tact, courtesy, which have limited and made graceful memoirs of all kinds, are seen in this kind of autobiography as enemies of truth. The more one commands the stage, the more one confesses, the greater the validity there will be in the experience. Protecting oneself or any other is cheating. It does make shocking and revelatory reading, when the author refuses to worry about self pity, self love, brutality and exposure, seeing them all as part of the natural human condition which has been whitewashed far too long.

Kate Millet puts her own work in the tradition of Violette Leduc, and certainly the portraits in *La Bâtarde* and *Mad in Pursuit* are often merciless as is Leduc's presentation of herself, wracked with self pity, envy, greed and paranoia. Their shared Catholic upbringing gives them a view of all people as essentially poor sinners incapable of their own salvation. Their shared loss of faith makes their obsessive confession more a raw exposure than a cleansing revelation.

Kate Millett sometimes debates presenting her story in fictional form, but it is never more than a question of defending herself against moral and legal claims made against her by the people she includes in her books.

Some of what has been left out of Anais Nin's published diaries was by request of the people she wrote about, though remarkably damaging material remains. Apparently some people felt it was better to be included unflatteringly than to be left out entirely. A few, of course, are dead, who cannot be slandered, having no legal rights. Some omissions are for Anais Nin's own protection of her privacy.

Surely, a central question for anyone writing autobiography is what to do with material which might be damaging either to the author or the other people in the book. The legal answer is getting permission from the victims of one's insight. Barring that, one writes, as Audrey Thomas does, changing the names of her characters. The moral question remains. Those willing to be exposed for the sake of being included still suffer pain. Those shallowly disguised are still perfectly recognizable and unprotected.

A friend of mine, contemplating an autobiographical story, said, "If the choice is between writing the story and living in harmony with my friends and neighbors, I won't hesitate to give up writing." Though such a view can be simply an excuse to avoid a difficult job, surely silence is a real moral choice.

To a large extent, it has been my own, based not so much on protecting myself and other people as on the freedom real fiction gives me to express all I understand without inhibition. In the process of publishing stories and novels, I have discovered there is no protection against readers who assign real identities to all my characters and assume I am all my main characters. I have been asked by academics to lecture on Yeats because another of my characters was a Yeats' scholar. I have been sent letters of sympathy for having only one arm. Because of a story I wrote about a couple my parents' age, a friend of my mother assumed that she had been pregnant before she married my father. Mother had the grace to be amused. If protection were the point, autobiography might be safer since at least I would be speaking the truth as I saw it, not burdening those close to me with false identities and experiences.

The point is, once the decision to write is made, there is no way to protect anyone. Any attempt to do so is not only doomed to failure but dangerously flaws the work. A fiction writer can claim to be innocent of intent to slander, but that's cold comfort for the victim. The autobiographical writer must believe that there is enough value in what is being said to justify whatever discomfort is caused.

Audrey Thomas says we are all each other's raw material. The reward she offers to those she has used in her work is the opportunity to use her in turn. She even proposes an anthology of stories about her, written by people who have appeared in her books, under the title, "Her Loyal Subjects." Not everyone has the talent for such retaliation. Those who do may not have the taste for it.

Telling the truth is not always either embarrassing or hurtful, but the writer of autobiography must face those extremes and come to some conclusions about them. Natalie Barney, notoriously confessional, considered that she was immortalizing lovers who might otherwise be in death forgotten, a fate she considered far worse than the minor irritation of invasion of privacy. She herself appeared in numbers of novels, poems, biographies as the arch lesbian of her time in Paris. There is no immorality for Kate Millet in celebrating her passionate and quarrelsome love of Sita, who lives now only in the book by her name. Audrey Thomas, addressing her latest character directly, says, "Remember, dear, the best revenge is writing well," a challenge, in this case, that may be taken up.

Autobiography and fiction are sourced in a universal need to know about oneself and other people, practiced in the low art of gossip ("Perhaps I can be forgiven if I suggest . . ." "I probably shouldn't tell you this, but . . .") by everyone. The only justification for transforming gossip into literature is writing well, which requires not only felicity of language but also true insight into what shouldn't be told but always is.

Morality in Literature

Morality has always been a major preoccupation in fiction. It may be more obvious in the preaching that has occurred in novels where the writer addresses the reader directly, cautions against the seductive power of certain characters, makes judgments on the purity of spirit or egotistical selfishness of the characters. Sometimes writers put their moral views into the thoughts and speech of particularly sympathetic characters. But the main and more powerful vehicle for morality is plot. Even in a thing made entirely of words, that old adage holds: "Action speaks louder than words." We judge people more by what they do than by what they say, and novelists have the further power of being able also to judge by what they make their characters do.

The human appetite for justice is so often thwarted in life that one of the chief activities of fantasy is to punish or reward those people who deserve but seem to receive neither in life. We are so frustrated by not only the lack of plot but also by lunatic accident that we invent heaven and hell to correct the meaninglessness and error in this world. When the majority of the population believed in after life, novelists felt freer than they do now to introduce justice even into otherwise realistic novels, rewarding good characters with happy marriages and riches, bankrupting, jailing, and killing off villains. Dickens, Austen and Thackeray were all writers of moral plots and taken seriously. Novels with moral plots today are usually classed as escape fiction. If we share a view of fate now, it is probably that the good will be victims and the villains will run the world.

Many of our finest contemporary novelists are leery of plot with its simplistic power of judgment, its illusions of moral cause and effect. They suspect righteousness itself, having seen millions dead in its name, wars interruptions of history which may finally destroy random life itself. But, if writers are often reluctant to judge, they are eager to understand, to perceive meaning in human experience, intuitive if not rational.

Even if novelists make no attempt to distort life into a moral tale, concern themselves with contemplating the random and accidental, any choice, any ordering will inevitably have moral meaning. That birth and death are accidents among many in between, few of which we deserve, doesn't relieve us of the business of leading our lives and, if we are novelists, our characters' lives through the valley of the shadow of death or any other landscape to some conclusion.

I have more often been called an immoral than a moral writer. So was D. H. Lawrence. So has any novelist been who has focused attention on the nature of sexuality. Even Margaret Laurence has been banned in the schools of Ontario. Yet sexual acts can have as much moral content as any other.

The first thing anyone asks at the birth of a baby is its sex. And from its birth most parents make distinctions in dress so that a stranger may know at a glance whether the child is a boy or a girl. Even in these days of unisex, my fifteen-month-old great niece wears a pink ribbon on her blue jean overalls. Though only intimate investigation could reveal sexual identity until puberty produces the real secondary sexual characteristics, we make sure the world knows whether our children are male or female in order that their education in those roles may begin at once. It is not, for the most part, an education in overt sexual behavior. Basically we distinguish between boys and girls to indicate to them which group will be expected to overthrow the authority of adults and take their place and which group will be expected to submit to that authority all their lives except as they act it out on the children of the next generation.

Probably in most cases we first perceive our fictional characters as male or female. Sometimes I may have question marks in early notebooks beside the sexes of children, but my adult characters present themselves to me first as men or women, heterosexual or homosexual, to be filled in and out from there.

Sex is the beginning of our identity, out of which most of us don't ever grow, even in the androgynous face of great age. What it means biologically, psychologically, culturally and politically is of basic importance to our understanding of anyone. Nothing we do is uncolored by that accident of birth. That its biological significance is highly exaggerated by our culture only makes it the more complex in its meaning. That we all, in one way or another, fail to comply with that cultural identity can be the source of the comedy or tragedy of life.

We use both statistical norms and cultural ideals as measures of all sorts. Sometimes they are in harmony. For instance, how tall an average woman is is probably how tall she also should ideally be, but how tall the average man is is not how tall he ideally should be. What influence these judgments have we can predict only in percentages of people, never for an individual; for, though we are rather large creatures to fit ourselves into the microcosm of atoms, we behave rather more like them than like objects in Newtonian physics. As individuals, we are random. That is, we can say that eighty percent of women who are 5'6" are happy about their height because they are both average and ideal, but we cannot know ahead of time how any particular individual woman of 5'6" will feel.

This is a simple, mildly interesting uncertainty in the making of character, and it is clearly related to sexuality, if only to underline that women are expected to be average, men to be superior not only to women but to each other.

At the center of sexuality, the norms and ideals are far more complex and conflicting. If there can be said to be norms at all, they are not arrived at in the ways we measure height or I.Q. Because sexual feeling and sexual behavior have been until very recently taboo subjects, we have only the primitive and faulty studies of Kinsey and his followers or the dream readings and speculations of Freudians to go by. Certainly none of this material provides the moral majority with the sort of average woman or average man they are looking for.

The nice girl and the honorable boy are fictions of the middle class. They are not norms at all, but ideals masquerading as norms, as is the innocence of childhood. Babies of both sexes masturbate. Boys are sexual braggarts and bullies. Girls are manipulators who give in unless they want to be social outcasts and then become social outcasts anyway. The real development of sexuality is naturally so out of kilter between the young of the two sexes, males at their peak of appetite in their teens, females reaching their zenith in their late twenties and early thirties, that it would take a sound and careful education in these differences to make kindly relations between them at all. The isolating of the sexes of the same age together is a barbarism of universal education that can't be confronted until we do admit that children are sexual, that their sexual development is different, that sexuality is at least as complex as toilet training, table manners, mathematics and grammar. We are sexual cretins not because sex is a primitive mystery or a moral outrage but because we have been left in ignorance of it.

What seems to me marvelous about the relatively recent acceptance of sexual explicitness in literature is that we finally have the opportunity to explore the complexities of sexuality, to educate ourselves and other people so that we at least have the opportunity to contemplate norms based on real facts, ideals that illuminate rather than blind love.

I am not concerned here with either pornography or erotic writing though both can teach us something about our real selves. Such fantasies reveal appetites for absolute power or absolute attention using sexual acts, among the most commonly shared real activities, as metaphors for those desires. In such writing the extremes of vanity are exposed. Pornography, particularly, is the great, inadvertent morality tale of our time.

The serious writer's job is not to segregate sexuality so that it may express only crude fantasy but to integrate sexuality with character for it to become one of the basic languages in which we can express our complex natures and communicate something far richer and more difficult than lust, not outside our morality but at its very center.

Lesbian and Writer

I am a politically involved lesbian, and I am a writer. I do not see the two as mutually exclusive; neither do I see them as inextricably bound together. Yet one of those two conflicting views is held by most people who read my work. The editors of *Chatelaine*, for instance, would as soon their readers weren't reminded that the writer of the Harry and Anna stories, affectionately and humorously concerned with family life, is also the author of *Lesbian Images*. Most critics of my novels, on the other hand, use my sexuality to measure all my characters. Those who are lesbian are naturally the most persuasive. My male characters are considered weak. Even for those not so crudely tempted, I am judged as remarkably fair to all my characters when one considers that I am, after all, a lesbian. For critics who are themselves gay, I am held politically accountable for every less than perfect gay character and am warned that I will lose a large part of my audience if I insist on including heterosexual characters in my work. And in the academy, I am dismissed as a marginal writer not because some of my characters share my sexuality but because I am a lesbian, therefore somehow mysteriously disqualified from presenting a vision of central value.

Kind, straight friends have argued that, if I weren't so visibly a lesbian, my work wouldn't be so often distorted and dismissed. But short of denying my sexuality, there is little I can do. It is not I but the interviewer or reviewer who is more interested in the fact that I am a lesbian than in the fact that I am a writer. My only positive choice under the circumstance is to use the media to make educational points about my sexuality.

Many people in the gay movement do not understand why I don't use my work as I am often willing to use myself for propaganda. Though one heterosexual critic did call *Lesbian Images* a piece of propaganda because in it I make my own bias quite clear, even that book does not satisfy the real propagandists who would have me not waste time on politically incorrect lesbian writers like Radcliffe Hall, May Sarton, Maureen Duffy—in fact, nearlly all the writers I studied in depth, but concentrate only on my most radical contemporaries, who are writing experimental erotica and separatist utopias.

I decided to be a writer not because I was a great reader as a child or had any natural gift for language but because I wanted to speak the truth as I saw it. To understand and share that understanding has been my preoccupation since I was in my teens. No political or moral ideal can supercede my commitment to portray people as they really are. What is is my domain. What ought to be is the business of politicians and preachers.

It is still a popular heterosexual belief that all homosexuals are at least sick and probably depraved, and they should, therefore, be, if not incarcerated in mental hospitals and jails, at least invisible. It is the conviction of gay militants that all homosexuals are victims and martyrs who must become heroically visible so that everyone will have to face the fact that education, industry, the law, medicine, and the government would all come to a grinding halt without the homosexuals who are the backbone of all our institutions. "Even Eleanor Roosevelt..." that argument can begin or end. The truth of experience lies elsewhere.

For offering a balanced view of society, I'm sure I know a disproportionate number of homosexuals, as I know a disproportionate number of artists, white people, Canadians. One of the truths about all of us is that we live in disproportionate groups. That is why novels tend to be full of Jews or blacks or soldiers or Englishmen or heterosexuals. Very few tend to be full of homosexuals because, until recently, homosexuals didn't live in social groups except in some places in Europe. My first two novels, *Desert of the Heart* and *This Is Not for You*, though they are about lesbian relationships, are not full of lesbians. I was writing about what was ardent, dangerous and secret, which is what lesbian experience still is for a great number of people. In my third novel, *Against the Season*, which was the beginning of my preoccupation with groups of people rather than with one or two main characters, out of about a dozen characters two are lesbian. There are a gay male and a lesbian in my fourth novel, *The Young in One Another's Arms*, out of a cast of about ten. Three and a half of eight characters are homosexual in my latest novel, *Contract with the World*. In all of my novels my gay characters move in an essentially heterosexual world as most gay people do. Though some of them are closeted in that world, some punished and defeated by it, they are all visible to the reader who is confronted with who they are and how they feel.

In a rare and beautiful comment about a character in *Contract with the World*, Leo Simpson says, "When Allen is arrested on some kind of homosexual charge, he has become so real that the laws of society immediately seem barbarous. Comfortable prejudices look like a tyranny of fear, which is of course part of what Rule's novel wants to say."

Yes, exactly, not heroic or saintly but *real*, and it is

part of what I want to say. But in this book I am basically
concerned with six or eight people, each of whom deals
with barbarous law and comfortable prejudice, not always
to do with homosexuality or even sexuality. What gathers
the characters into one book is their involvement with art
in a provincial city far from any cultural center. To be an
artist in this country is very difficult. To deal with the pain
and doubt and wonder of such aspirations is my chief preoccupation in this book. My characters are neither necessarily greatly talented nor superior in vision simply because
they are artists. They all have to face the fact that, except
for the few greatest, artists are considered failures. A great
many very gifted or not, can't stand such a climate. In this
they share something of the strain it is to be homosexual
in a homophobic culture.

I owe to my own art all the honesty and insight I have,
not simply about homosexuals and artists, both of which I
happen to be, but about the whole range of my experience
as a member of a family, a community, a country. I don't
write Harry and Anna stories to cater to *Chatelaine's* heterosexual readers though I like the cheques well enough when
they come in. (No one could eat writing for *Christopher
Street*, and I still give most of my short fiction away.) I
write them out of affection for those men and women,
like my own parents, who care for and love and enjoy their
children and because I, too, have cared for and loved and
enjoyed children. There are heterosexual men and women
in all my work because there are heterosexual men and
women in my life and world, to whom I owe much of my
understanding.

A blind writer once said to me, "You're the only writer
I know who includes characters who happen to be physically
handicapped. In most fiction, if they are there at all, it's
because they're handicapped." That for me is the real distinction between what I write and propaganda. I am trying to
make the real visible. People 'happen to be' a lot of things

about which there are cultural phobias. I have never found either safety or comfort in a blind heart, as a way to work or live.

As a lesbian, I believe it is important to stand up and be counted, to insist on the dignity and joy loving another woman is for me. If that gets in the way of people's reading my books, I have finally to see that it is their problem and not mine. As a writer, I must be free to say what is in all the diversity I can command. I regret the distorting prejudices that surround me, whether they affect homosexuals or men or the physically handicapped, and I can't alone defeat them. They will not defeat me, either as a lesbian or a writer.

For "Writer/Publisher Relationships:
Feminist and Traditional"

When I began to write, I was not interested in little magazines or small presses. Like a lot of young daydreamers, I wanted my stories in *Atlantic Monthly* or *The New Yorker,* neither of which I've appeared in to this day. The publishers I considered worthy were those who published writers I admired, firms like Little Brown and Hogarth Press. Oh, I might have considered little mags if they were *The Paris Review* or *The London Magazine,* but I had no concept of working toward such goals. Either what I wrote was good enough or it wasn't. To add to the unreality of those ambitions, I had a horror of being published by anyone I really knew, having any favors done me by writers already known. In those pre-women's movement days, I called my plans "wanting to play with the big boys," a hangover from a childhood of tagging after an older brother whose activities always seemed more interesting than my own.

Ten unpublished years later, a story of mine was accepted for the anthology, *Klanak Islands,* published by a small press in Vancouver, run by Alice and Bill McConnell, friends of mine. Another was accepted for CBC *Anthology*, recommended by another friend who was the west coast editor.

Publishing my first novel (really my third—the first two are still in a bottom drawer) came a little closer to my expectations. MacMillan of Canada accepted it if I could get a British or American publisher as well. In those easier days, I did have both English and American agents. When Secker and Warburg accepted the book in England, I was delighted. What I did not know was that Secker and Warburg provided neither editor nor copy editor. The book was published, spelling mistakes and all, after solicitors had carefully checked it for libel and the printer had questioned one remark as possibly offensive to the Queen. MacMillan of Canada bought pages.

Most large houses in the States have editors, and I've had excellent help from them at McCall Publishing, at Doubleday and at Harcourt, Brace, Jovanovich. I have also been paid respectable advances. The difficulty about working with a large American house is that often no one but the book's editor gives a damn about the book and that editor rarely has the clout to get advertising money, sales representative enthusiasm, and must be resigned to the fact that the firm has no ambitions for most books but to break even. The only way to force the firm's interest is to command a very large advance they have to earn back, but, before you can do that, you've had to prove your earning power, and most writers are never given that chance. If the first printing sells out in three or four months, no plans are made for reprinting unless there is enormous pressure from bookstores. Routinely bookstores don't risk large second orders unless a publicity campaign is in place to support new sales. They wait for the paperback.

The trouble with mass paperback publishers is that they buy rights for five years, and, unless they've had to pay a very high amount for those rights, they often issue the book once or twice in that period when it is available everywhere for about six weeks and then out of print.

The marketing of books as if they were like food, stale after six months if they are hardbacks, after six weeks if they are paperbacks, is the general practice of large publishers. Not only does this give a book too short a shelf life for the only advertising it gets, word of mouth from people who have enjoyed reading it, but it also makes its use in classrooms impossible. It isn't around long enough for teachers to order it.

The great virtue of the small presses who manage to stay afloat is that they maintain their back lists so that a book may be available to its audience for some years rather than some months. While few of these presses can afford the advances large companies offer, they often, in the long run, make a good deal more for their authors.

Very few small presses have a staff with the range of talents necessary to produce books that are well edited and well designed, to handle secondary rights and distribution as successfully as they should.

Nobody in Canada designs handsomer books than Talonbooks, but they have no professionally trained editors, and they've turned over their distribution to the University of Toronto Press, whose reputation is for very uneven service.

Feminist presses suffer the same limitations, but they have advantages over many other sorts of small presses. They have a growing network of bookstores all over North America who specialize in their books. They often sell large numbers of books through direct mail order, and their customers are people for whom books are important sources of nourishment, who buy books even when they can't afford to go out to dinner. Also other women with skills volunteer them. People also volunteer to do some of the routine work of the business.

After years of "playing with the big boys," I have opted for publishing with Naiad, a lesbian/feminist press in the States, run by Barbara Grier whom I've known for twenty years. She used to be editor of *The Ladder,* the only lesbian magazine in the States through the 50s and 60s. Naiad can't afford to pay advances, has no editor, an apprentice book designer who is improving. What they do have is a team of two people determined to sell books. They fill orders the day they receive them. They go to every feminist and lesbian conference, every book fair, and the books they sell are never allowed to go out of print.

I work for a better standard of cover, offer suggestions, find images for them to use. I have already edited one book for them and will work on others until they can afford to pay for editorial help. I find writers I think Naiad should publish. I can't turn myself into a media star, the only help the establishment publishers know how to use, but there is a lot I can do for Naiad to make not only my books but all their books better looking, more readable and more widely known.

I'm sure there will be problems, but I feel confident about being able to solve most of them because I'm working with people whose goals are the same as mine. They want their books not only in the stores but in the classrooms, easily and continuously available to everyone who wants them. They want to make a living for themselves and for their writers.

I have dealt so far only with the practical problems of publishing. Writers suspect that the aims of large American publishers operate against certain kinds of books. It is my experience that the only criterion for large publishers is what they think they can sell. That their promotions and sales departments routinely desert all but a couple of best-sellers each season is one of the mysteries. Books are not rejected because they have Canadian settings, homosexual characters, four-letter words. They are rejected because a company doesn't think it can sell them. Books are, for instance, routinely rejected for being too well written to be popular. Some houses accept a few "literary" books each year to keep up their image. They don't know how to market and therefore claim literary works can't be marketed. Books are accepted by large U.S. and Canadian houses because their authors can be marketed, either already well known as public personalities or good looking and articulate enough to become media favorites.

Large publishers in the States have not neglected feminist issues because books like Kate Millet's *Sexual Politics* sold very well. I have noticed that nonfiction and fiction with an autobiographical, confessional tone have had more encouragement than political novels and novels of ideas. It is left to the feminist presses to publish those, and there are an increasing number of very good ones, well worth the effort of keeping them in print. They are novels about collective living, feminist businesses, rape relief centres and battered wife shelters, about children growing up with lesbian mothers. Because thousands of women are confronting these issues in their own lives, there is a growing audience for such books. I suspect when several have become really popular, large publishers will begin to reconsider them.

Only small publishers have ever risked publishing really radical writing, whether it is political, philosophical or erotic. The feminist press carries on that tradition and opens the field to women's voices raising some issues men have often not wanted discussed, from their death-wish politics to their death-wish sexuality.

Even if there are virtues in publishing with the establishment, some feminists argue that publishing with anyone but a feminist press is politically incorrect. The horror stories of those who have chosen feminist presses simply because they were feminist (or claimed to be) without looking at the very practical problems involved, without asking questions like whether or not they'd survive to publication day, whether or not they intended to honor their royalty commitments, should warn writers that a feminist label is in itself not much to go by. People like Rita Mae Brown have been so burned as to avoid feminist presses entirely. To offer oneself up as a victim to political enthusiasms alone seems to me irresponsible to one's own work. There are only so many good feminist publishing houses, and they can't publish all that is being written in that area. If an establishment publisher will take a book that a feminist press won't, it would seem to me foolish not to take advantage of being published, for the writer's first responsibility is to reach her audience.

I have published everywhere I could, whether in *The Globe and Mail* or *The Body Politic, Redbook* or *Sinister Wisdom*. Though I would like always to publish both in Canada and the United States, I don't turn down an American offer if Canadian publishers either aren't interested or don't make reasonable offers. It does not seem to me politically sane to be silenced rather than publish in the "wrong" places. In fact, writing in the wrong places is often important to reach an audience that needs to hear different views.

The danger of putting politics above all other consideratins is greater for publishers than for writers. I heard one feminist publisher say that she had decided to publish nothing but what was politically correct and for a year didn't publish anything because works of literature judged politically always failed somewhere. If feminist publishers take a narrow political line, they will be the worst rather than the best places for writers to publish because they would have become propagandists rather than tellers of the truth. Narrow zeal and censorship go hand in hand.

I'm glad to say, at Naiad anyway, the editorial position is pragmatic. Those 50s lesbian romances aren't all that liberated, but the nostalgia for those bad, old days makes them popular. They can help support books less popular but in the long run more important. While Naiad opens its doors for the minorities within its minority, it doesn't at the same time forbid major heterosexual content in its books, and it has no prejudice against members of the white middle class or even the rich.

No book really worth reading tells you only what you

want to know about yourself as well as the world you live in. It's the courage to write and publish that sort of literature and the freedom to do it that feminist publishers can best guard and serve.

Playing with the women instead of the big boys is an ambition I hope the writers of coming generations will recognize and fulfill.

For the Critic of What Isn't There

The guilt-tripping criticism of politically correct feminists does not come from third world women who demand simply the right to speak for themselves. It comes from guilty middle-class white women who mistakenly think they can help their less fortunate sisters by insisting other people like themselves speak for the less privileged. They urge writers to take the time to understand third world and poor women enough to include them in their cast of characters, to make them "visible." In that attitude I hear the same condescension I have heard in charitable good works of junior league mentality which have always done more for the conscience of the do-gooders than for improving the condition of those receiving charity. It assumes their helplessness and perpetuates it.

To argue that the experience of those less materially fortunate, culturally alienated is more worthy of record is to sentimentalize and trivialize real experience which has its own strong, eloquent voice. What arrogance it would be for any white woman to assume that she should be writing Audre Lorde's life instead of Audre Lorde herself! To co-opt someone else's pain and strength for our own moral improvement is obscene plagiarism, and yet it is extolled as the way to restore innocence and health to the white middle class.

Charity is a cop-out so traditionally female in its apparent self-effacement that there seems resonant comfort in it. We're no longer supposed to serve the imaginations of the men who have dominated us. We are to give up ourselves instead to those whose suffering is greater than our own. Looking down is just as distorting as looking up and as dangerous in perpetuating hierarchies.

There is no reason for women to feel any guilt about being white or middle class unless they are abusing those privileges. Perhaps the greatest misuse women make of any advantage they have is not to use it at all, to allow themselves instead to feel unworthy, ashamed, therefore denying the responsibility of good fortune. They seem to be saying there is nothing wrong with the advantages themselves, but only the poor deserve them.

Guilt is a classic middle-class, female sin dressed up as a virtue, and our poorer sisters know it. They sass us with what they could do with the bit of money, the bit of leisure we command, ghetto shrewd, honoring their lives enough to fight for them. Kids I know who started out on welfare are figuring out how to get federal grants to paint, write, film, sing this world into new meanings.

Working-class as well as middle-class women with business savvy are founding presses, bookstores, art galleries, film companies, and women are supporting their own enterprises. Naiad Press, for instance, reports a 180% growth for 1982 and wonders what it could be like in "good times." They publish books by middle-class women, third-world women, ex-nuns and escapist romancers. Donna Deitch has raised enough money to make a film meaningful to women by selling shares to other women. Judy Baca is painting the longest mural in the world, the hidden history of California, on municipal, state and federal grants, on private donations. Even the Olympics Committee and the army are involved.

"The Dinner Party," against all financial odds, shows to record crowds in every city and has been written about more than any other event in art. Energy for these kinds of major accomplishments isn't born of guilt.

For those white, middle-class critics who would turn their own writers into the foolish virgins of parable, without any light of their own for the dark which everyone shares, I would suggest that the practice of reading for what isn't there is ultimately to see no one, not the Brontës, not George Eliot, not Virginia Woolf, not Gertrude Stein, the list goes on and on.

What I know I share with all women is the potential courage to speak for myself and the capacity to listen, to bear and be witness. I can serve no one's life experience and imagination but my own. To deny its value is to squander what gift I have. My job is not to speak for other people but to listen to them speaking for themselves to expand my understanding of what it is to be human and female at the end of the 20th century.

Staking Out the Territory

A university student in British Columbia, reading for the first time the descriptions of the British Columbia forest by Emily Carr, said, "That's what the forest is, all right. I wonder what it would be like to read Wordsworth if you were English." It is a quite ordinary experience for children in many places in North America to grow up without ever reading anything with a setting familiar to them, never to experience the wonder of that particular recognition, confirmation of reality, until they are adults choosing their own books, that is, if they still read. Young North American writers have been drawn to England and Europe because, in their literary experience, only those places are real.

Perhaps the reason why the vast majority of people with homosexual tastes have had to marry and fail at marriage before they could establish relationships meaningful to them is that heterosexuality like Europe has been the only reality in literature. The few lesbian classics like *The Well of Loneliness* and *Nightwood* held up mirrors distorting enough to frighten and discourage most women neither male identified nor given to drugged hallucinations.

As a dyslexic child of six (called a slow reader in those unenlightened days), I may have suffered more severely than most from feelings of alienation from the world of print. I did not want to identify with Jane in *The Dick and Jane Reader* to "see Dick run." My brother's name was Arthur, and I ran with him. The books read to me at home were either fantasies or animal stories. I discounted the first from my princeless world and resisted the second since my mother did not approve of pets. "Bring home any stray you want as long as it's human."

I read a Nancy Drew mystery or two, but I was into my teens pretty much a non-reader except for what was required of me in school. I loathed books like *Ivanhoe*, and I finally finished *David Copperfield* in funnybook form. Even my first experience of Shakespeare left me to understand that the women were really young boys, and that was why there was so much fooling around with boys pretending to be girls pretending to be boys.

Literature was either not about any world I knew and needed to understand, or it was hypocritical as so many of the adults around me seemed to be. The first serious writing I did, to expose the misuse of student funds by the principal, was used to expel me from school.

I arrived at college passionate to be a writer in order to tell the *truth*, an illiterate sixteen-year-old with scorn for nearly every written word but my own. I read avidly after that only as a means of learning my craft. Since moral, political and cultural issues were beside the point in literary discussions, I could concentrate on the technical and aesthetic issues useful to me in my own work. I learned to ignore subject matter entirely for the joys of language itself. Even reading Milton could be a pleasure. I forgot that I had been angry about the lies literature told until years later when I read Kate Millet's *Sexual Politics* which put me back in touch with a rage I had learned to bury against all the ugly propaganda about women. I could not read without anger for months.

With such a background, I am bewildered about questions concerning literary influences on my work. I spent the first years of my writing life trying to shake off Dickens, Thackeray, Henry James, Jane Austen, Hemingway, who had never been anything but aliens in my mind, voices against my own spirit and vision.

It didn't occur to me to look, because I didn't believe I would find, writers doing what I wanted to do. I must have been thirty before I picked up a copy of Dorothy Baker's *Cassandra at the Wedding*. It was the first book I had ever read even remotely like the work I was trying to do in setting, in tone, in emotional climate, and my reaction was not one of joyful recognition but of alarm. I had been alone too long to know what to do with literary company, I was perversely relieved to find that an earlier book of hers, *Trio*, was badly distorted by homophobia.

Not until I was commissioned to write *Lesbian Images* did I really read a range of novels by or about lesbians. It is hard to know how many of those writers would have been models for me if I had been introduced to them as a student. I enormously admire Willa Cather, but I rather think her dependence on male narrators to express her protective tenderness toward women would have struck me as a dishonest device in my morally simplistic teens. Even Gertrude Stein and Virginia Woolf felt required to disguise rather than illuminate passionate relationships between women.

It is not, of course, only in relationships with women that I'm interested in telling the truth, but a literary tradition which excludes so central an experience for me is one to be generally mistrusted. I am fairly hard pressed to find truths about relationships between men and women either, since women were obviously frightened by what they knew and men ignorant or indifferent.

There is some real virtue in feeling morally detached from a literary tradition, and by now it is detached rather than alienated that I feel. A great many young writers are overwhelmed by what has already been said and take a long time to locate their own territory. Mine was waiting for me even in my childhood.

The first mappers had been there before me, and I have learned to be grateful for them when their efforts were necessarily sometimes crude, timid, or mistaken. Homesteading an emotional territory as I have takes a lot of simple hard work. I can regret a lack of elegance sometimes, sacrificed to the urgent necessity to be clear. But, if we are to have a civilized literature, the bush has to be cleared first, the basic necessities of life supplied.

As a homesteader, I live a fair distance from other writers in the territory. They are for me like the "ironic points of light" in Auden's "September, 1939." I have not only overcome my first fear of them but feel relief and gratitude that others share the work with me. There are enough of us now that we don't need always to be writing about suffering and isolation. Even in the bad, old days we are discovering that some of us led richly nourishing and productive lives, but we must never forget the human damage silence and lies have caused. What we have to say must sting as well as sing if we are to open the territory for those who come after us. I want to be sure from the faint tracings I inherited, I leave at least a hard bed, a comfortable rocking chair, a warm hearth, and a few of the survival skills I've learned. I want to have created a place that is real, in which it is not only possible but often joyful to live.

PART II:

WRITING FOR THE GAY PRESS

Why I Write for *The Body Politic*

Gay friends of mine, both men and women who like
me have established themselves in various professions like
teaching, writing, the law, often question my involvement
with *The Body Politic*, a paper they read only intermittently,
about which they are nervously ambivalent. They are quick
to criticise, to focus on issues they themselves would not
support like sexual relationships between adults and children, sexual activity in bars and baths. They consider such
behavior exactly what makes it difficult for people like
themselves to be accepted, for, as long as they are identified with those extremes of sexual behavior, they feel unable
to argue their right to be in positions of responsibility for
children, for sick people, for people in difficulty with the
law. Many of them are at odds with their churches and
neighborhoods and political parties only in the fact of
their sexual preference and are at pains to prove they are
in all ways as responsible as other citizens for the moral
health of their communities. If they do belong to groups
advocating social change, they tend to choose humanitarian
ventures like Save the Children and Oxfam or causes like

Amnesty International which to date excludes their own. They argue that their sexuality should be a private matter: to make it a public issue would be to distort its importance to themselves as well as the world they live in.

But then they do agree that they feel guilty, too, at not doing something or something more to change the climate for homosexuals. But they really don't see how I can appear in a paper whose policy is to advertise and support sexual behavior which can only damage the homosexual image in the eyes of the majority and increase prejudice against us. Since my personal life seems so much like theirs, they really would like to know why, and I try to tell them.

Neither sexual liberation between men and boys nor the baths are priorities of my own, obviously. Though I am perfectly willing to listen to Gerald Hannon's extolling the pleasures of sexual toys like whips and nipple clips, I will continue to have reservations about the celebration of master/slave games, not because they are kinky but because they are all too normal, not to say reactionary. The political value of his argument for me remains. Until our right to consenting sexual acts is established, limited only by the rights of others, no homosexual behavior will be protected because anything any of us does is offensive to the majority. Policing ourselves to be less offensive to that majority is to be part of our own oppression. Tokenism has never been anything else.

By writing for *The Body Politic*, I refuse to be a token, one of those who doesn't really seem like a lesbian at all. If the newspaper is found to be obscene, I am part of that obscenity. And proud to be, for, though my priorities and the paper's aren't always the same, I have been better and more thoughtfully informed about what it is to be homosexual in this culture by *The Body Politic* than by any other paper, offered information the straight press refuses to publish whether about John Damien's case or the legal niceties of crossing the border or the prospect of our being in human rights codes across Canada. I am kept informed about our scholars, artists, politicians, as well as our victims and fighters. Most of the people I know who don't read *The Body Politic* regularly are dangerously ignorant about what is actually going on either here or abroad.

While too many homosexuals nervously debated the bad taste and/or bad timing of the article "Men Loving Boys/ Loving Men," a number of heterosexuals acknowledged both the value of *The Body Politic* and the importance of the issue when they took out an ad in *The Globe and Mail*, asking that obscenity charges be dropped. That statement was important, and it did impress some homosexuals that people like Margaret Atwood and June Callwood thought *The Body Politic* worth defending.

Whether we like it or not, our sexuality isn't a private matter, and the altruism of some good citizens hasn't changed the government's mind. What will change the social climate is our own persistence, through silence or bigotry in the straight press, government sponsored court cases, and police raids, to gain our rights. *The Body Politic* has a proud history and future in that battle.

Extended Care

Popular magazines, once every five years or so, usually in their medical columns, assure us that some people in their fifties, sixties, and even seventies are still sexually active. I never had any doubt of it. One grandfather had four wives, his youngest son the same age as his first great-grandson, and he was contemplating yet another marriage just a year before he died at ninety-one. My other grandfather stored pictures of his young secretaries in bathing suits loose in family albums, from which they fluttered out onto the laps of innocent browsers. I haven't such evidence from my grandmothers. One was enormous and badly arthritic by the time she was fifty, neglected by her husband and certainly not in the market for lovers, but she suspected the worst of nearly everyone else. The other was by her own admission frigid, though in her dying months all her delusions were sexual whether about the activities of her aging nurse or the neighborhood cats.

We are sexual creatures all our lives in a culture which accepts our sexuality only from puberty to menopause or a foolish bit longer for men whose physical stages aren't as

dramatically marked. Sexual activity not linked with procreation is perverse whether it is between children, people
of the same sex, or old people. There has been a marked
change in attitude, except among conservative Catholics,
for acceptance of sexual pleasure as a good in itself. Mastur-
bation as an aid to self knowledge or a physical relief is
encouraged for frigid women and men in the service. But
that most universal sexual practice is still forbidden to
children and the scandal of nursing homes.

What marks all homosexuals as rebels, whether we feel
all that rebellious or not, is our refusal to accept the narrow
categories of sexual activity dictated by our culture. Many
of us simply want to be left alone as consenting adults in
the privacy of our own beds. Others of us, pariahs from
the start, develop a sexual recklessness not always either
wise or admirable. I don't think we've yet said very much
that is anything but indulgently self-serving about either
children's sexuality or sado-masochism. I can credit us only
with being willing to discuss such subjects at all. About
sexuality and aging, gay men are probably worse than the
dominant culture, and there are only a few women like
May Sarton who speak to the long range of life, the fact
of dying. Locked in defiant breaking of taboos, we don't
very often take a long, considered view of what our sexuality
is and how it is best to use it, variously, all our lives.

Not only does the importance of sexual experience differ
from person to person but even more importantly it alters
for each person at different stages of living, influenced
also by health, by circumstance, by changing perception.
We must stop arguing absolutely even for fixed homosexuality, never mind particular sexual practices, and open
to an understanding of change throughout our lives.

Preoccupation with periods of intense sexual activity
as the goal of liberation, simply because it is the image of
immorality, can become finally not only boring but distorting in a damaging way of how we read the length of
our lives. It's akin to that view that, once you can't play

football, your only option is to sit in front of the tv with a bottle of beer or whiskey, and it surely in part accounts for the popularity of pornographic films, watched so often in lonely motel rooms across the continent not by people preparing for assault and rape but simply too old and tired to compete in the sexual marketplace. I suspect at least some of the brutality against women and victimizing of young men plays to the anger of aging people at their being no longer acceptable sexual partners.

Some old people confront the sexual repression of their earlier lives with a need to rage against it. Yeats came to sexual fierceness at the edge of the grave. Heterosexual women, discarded because of their age, would be well advised to go some place like the West Indies where such sexual vitality is admired rather than laughed at.

There is bafflement for people no longer all that interested in either the athletics of sex or its conquests, not only because they are physically limited but because their psychic needs are different. The gentler eroticism of people no longer very often sexually active is either unacknowledged or mocked as much in the homosexual as in the heterosexual world.

My grandfather of the voluptuous secretaries was delighted to be a substitute father, give them away in marriage, and he adored a niece, a granddaughter, writing them candid love letters without a notion of proposing incest. Yet he courted them as surely—perhaps more surely—than he had sexually courted women as a young man.

Recently I watched a southern grandmother, surrounded by her young in the brief dress of that humid summer climate. She loved their bare thighs, the backs of their necks, their ears, touched and caressed the babies, the children, the adolescents. When I commented on how physically affectionate she was, an otherwise very shy adolescent grandson said, "Why, you have to kiss grandma good-by when you go to the bathroom."

Mocking distaste of the old is as much a part of disgust

for the body as ugly attitudes toward other kinds of sexuality. Its source is fear of death. The body finally betrays us, and in the old we witness the signs of that betrayal. We'd be well advised to spend far less time defending orgiastic and sado-masochistic behavior, attempts to unite pain and pleasure into a higher ecstasy, and far more time carefully distinguishing between those two physiologically related sensations to make us better lovers in old age. *The Grapes of Wrath* was a novel seen as unfit for high school students because in it a young woman offers her milk-filled breast to a dying old man. Of course, it is erotic as well as humane behavior. Uniting the two is what shocked people. Yet surely intimacy with our own and other bodies should teach us exactly that. Now we seem content to leave such understanding to nurses in old people's homes. I heard an old woman weep in wonder that a young nurse would use her own hands lovingly to serve an ailing bowel. For me there is more revoltionary wonder in that than in fist-fucking. Given the impersonality of much revolting zeal, I'd be less surprised to be encouraged to follow Hemingway into necrophilia than Steinbeck into erotic tenderness for old age in its lusts and pains, its beauty and fragility.

Women traditionally have had to tend the young, the sick and the old and are more prepared to accept and expand their erotic tenderness against the prevailing horror of aging. Lesbians in particular, not interested in serving men's fear of aging by dying our own hair and having our faces lifted, are free to refuse to take that bigotry into our own lives, and free to challenge our gay brothers who are at least as guilty as straight men in mocking and fearing the old. In this, Yeats is wrong. An aging man is not "a paltry thing, a tattered coat upon a stick." I heard Leonard Cohen at a reading of his erotic poetry say to a Picasso-headed old man in the audience, "I know you disapprove of me, but you're old, you'll be dead soon." At the end of the reading, that old man laid a hand on Leonard Cohen's arm and said, "I am an old man who loves you." In old age, we must have reached the confidence to speak our hearts.

A fairly popular button in lesbian circles says, "I like older women." How about "Bald is beautiful?" Though men rarely believe it, a great many women, I among them, really think so. Why shouldn't other men? I have a t shirt, given me on my fiftieth birthday, which reads, "Once you're over the hill, you pick up speed." It's true for very few of us, certainly not for me, but coasting some after the long, hard climb has its real pleasures. Since I have always had a taste for older women, I don't mind being one. In fact, I celebrate age, flaunt it, if you like. When I titled my column "So's Your Grandmother," I wasn't kidding. If we really want to change the world, let's celebrate the sexual connotations of "extended care."

Hindsight

Gore Vidal calls himself a homosexualist rather than a homosexual, insisting that it is a taste and activity being described, not a person. I'm not taken with the word, but I'm taken with the point. In our new pride and political zeal we commit ourselves too narrowly not only to who we are but also to what we do.

It is surely hindsight that makes some people say, "Oh, I knew I was homosexual by the time I was six." But I suspect it is also hindsight at sixteen, or thirty or even sixty. We know by past experience what our tastes are. I even understand what people mean who in old age without any homosexual experience claim, nevertheless, to be homosexual, aware of life-long desires they haven't had the courage to act on. Those same people would not, I think, call themselves mountain climbers if they'd never climbed a mountain, novelists if they'd never written a book.

Few people who call themselves homosexual have not had heterosexual experience, often extensive experience, and it needn't seem either at the time or later unpleasant or unhappy. Not all married people with homosexual tastes are simply hiding in heterosexuality. Vita Sackville-West, except in moments of lunatic passion, wanted to be married to her husband, and his taste for boys didn't diminish his love for her.

I sometimes suspect it's the moral and political climate of heterosexuality as much as physical appetite that makes some of us cultivate our homosexual desires while we let whatever faint sparks of heterosexual desire die for lack of imaginative fuel.

Sexual appetite, like all appetites, is not fixed. As our bodies, our needs, and our knowledge grow and change, so do our choices, if not of partners, certainly of practices. Sex for a healthy nineteen-year-old may make up in athletic prowess what it lacks in subtlety. What passes for sex in some old people may be too subtle to be identified by the blatant young. Most people in long term, monagamous relationships, after the first few years, are sexually semi-retired, sometimes happily so, sometimes only fitfully rest-less. Being married is always expressed as a passive state, by men and women alike. And it may for a time or a life-time seem a blessedly safe shore after the sexual turbulence of being single.

Most of us have been obsessively sexual at some period or periods of our lives, not always coinciding with the age we are supposed to be for such hyperactivity. There are probably as few great sexualists of whatever persuasion as there are great violinists or novelists because most of us are unwilling to practice those hours a day that it takes and anyway don't have the native talent or stamina. If our sexual tastes were not stigmatized, we would spend far less time defending them and relatively more time learning to understand and enjoy them in balance with all the other tastes which nourish us as human beings.

"What is all the fuss?" demanded a disillusioned nineteen-year-old. "It doesn't even take as long as a game of tennis," and then she fell in love. But she may ask the question again and have it differently answered. A woman in her sixties who last year said she was glad to be through with all that is now passionately involved in a new relationship.

One of the great reassurances for me is that most of us can get ourselves out of the boxes we put ourselves into if the need is there. W. H. Auden said he was a poet only when he was writing a poem. We don't yet have the political freedom to be able to be homosexuals only when we are making love with members of our own sex, but it is that freedom I know I'm working for. I may have to go on calling myself a lesbian into great old age, not because it is any longer true but because it takes such a long time to make the simple point that I have the right to be. I hope that I can at least keep that distinction clear for myself so that I am in touch with who I really am in every phase of my life. Then, when someone asks, "What are you trying to prove?," I'll remember to make a political speech rather than a sexual overture . . . unless, of course, I feel like it.

Free to Live

My little grandmother who had everything wrong with her, arthritis, phlebitis, anemia, to say nothing about her nerves, said to me, "The one thing I don't want to do is lose my mind. As long as I have my mind . . ." She used it mostly for playing cards, the horses, memorizing the words to her favorite songs, and bugging my mother. Nevertheless, she thought her mind was important to her. And she did, in the last year of her life, lose it. At first she only wrote cheques on banks where she didn't have accounts and phoned us in cities where we didn't live, but gradually hallucinations took over her days and nights, mostly in bizarre sexual forms. Then she was convinced she was in a motel or rest home or hospital, and she begged to be taken home, not to the house where she then, in fact, lived, but to her childhood home, to her parents, sisters and brother. Reclusive as a result of illness and fear, she hadn't gone out socially for years. People kept sending her invitations because she refused them with flowers. Now, after twenty years, she began to accept those invitations, and members of the family had to take her to garden and cocktail parties of the retired military, the garden club. She swung in on the arm of a grandchild, wielding her cane, found a place to sit and raffled off the cherry in her Old Fashioned to other bemused and ailing old people.

Once, on the way home from one of those parties, she said to me, "Do you remember how I used to say to you I was afraid of losing my mind?"

"Yes," I answered cautiously.

"Well, it's not so bad," she replied. "I think, is that the world I was afraid of for all those years? Is that all it is?"

Divorced when it was not the thing to be divorced, married a second time to an alcoholic she wouldn't divorce because a second time round would prove she was at fault, my little grandmother had to lose her mind to lose her shame, to be free of all that social garbage. Her last night of consciousness, she sang every song she'd ever known, and my mother sang with her, everything from "Dixie Dan, ambling, rambling, gambling minstral man" to "You'll Never Walk Alone" and "To Kiss in the Sunlight," two favorites of mine as well, since I was also afraid of my loneliness and the secrecy imposed upon my heart.

As I watch so many of my friends reclusive in fear, defending their silence and lies, I understand that I am, in an odd way, my little grandmother gone crazy, not to be free to die but to be free to live. I want to say, in my turn, "It's not so bad. The terrifying, judgmental world out there isn't all it's cracked up to be. It can be maneuvered with a kid and a cane." Because of my little grandmother, I didn't wait to be lame as I sometimes am now to walk in the world. Her beloved bad example sent me crazy brave when I still walked without help. Like her, I was afraid, and I fell, broke courage, bones, but, because of her, I knew it was my fear that crippled, nothing else.

Nearly everything that I was once deathly afraid of has happened to me. I lost a beloved woman to her moral scruples. No one would publish my work for ten years, and I was nearly as frightened of my eventual success as I was of my failure. When my third novel was finally accepted by a publisher, I had no idea how much of my world I was risking. I kept my teaching job. Of my family, only my younger sister wanted to disown me for a while. The several friends I lost were gay and afraid to be seen any longer in my company.

I had published several novels and *Lesbian Images* before national magazines began doing profiles of me, ostensibly because I am a writer, but really because I am a lesbian. Every time one of these comes out, I get letters, hate mail, cries for help, love letters, religious tracts. Many more people read journalistic junk than they do books. The greatest horror for most closeted people is to be publicly exposed, never again to be known as a writer or teacher or parent but always to be identified as a lesbian and therefore discredited.

The fear is far worse than the fact. Even the polls say that over fifty percent of Canadians think gay people should have civil rights, and most people don't care much one way or the other. The parents it would kill live on, and siblings gradually gain new tolerance and understanding. Each year the sexual orientation clause is added to another union contract. If all else fails, there are always jobs at the post office.

The benefits are enormous. Once the very worst has happened, there's nothing left to be afraid of that isn't the common lot. The energy that fed anxiety can be turned instead to work, to love, to telling the truth, whose ring is very sweet after years of silence and lying. If there is an anticlimax in finding that one is not, after all, a martyr, but in the words of one of our since dead national magazines, "simply a human being," it is a letdown we can live with happily. "Is that all it is?" my little grandmother asked. That's all.

Walking Canes

Back in 1959, when Helen and I bought our first house, my parents were tactfully silent, but the man at the government mortgage office did everything he could to discourage us. Helen was teaching in the English Department at UBC, and I was Assistant Director of International House. Our combined salaries comfortably qualified us for a mortgage, but didn't we see that we were only two women, and how could two women take on the responsibility and *commitment* of owning a house together? Children of friends told us their parents thought we were both too attractive to give up so easily.

Helen had owned houses before and very much wanted to be out of the apartment I had rented when she brought her furniture out from the east. I loathed that place even more than she did, the smell of other people's cooking taking away my appetite, the blank wall where there should have been a view of the sea and mountains, the unused plug in the fake fireplace. But, if I had been alone to see to my own comfort, I would have looked for a comfortable room in someone else's house, not for a house of my own. I was both domestically retarded and afraid of being tied down with physical and financial responsibilities.

It is, of course, easier to own a house, once it is affordable. You don't have to carry your belongings about with you every time you want to go anywhere or pay to have them stored. We traveled far more easily than we had before. Once we swapped both houses and cars with a woman in London and had three months in England for the price of the plane tickets.

We ougrew that first house. The second, after ten years, outgrew us when Helen wanted to retire early, and we both wanted to live on the island we'd already chosen for weekends and holidays. After living with Helen for nearly thirty years, I can still be surprised at our mobility and our capacity to change direction as our needs change.

Relationships, like houses, can be outgrown or can outgrow the people involved. Like houses, they can become too small or too expensive. We aren't inclined to think of houses left behind as failures unless we were duped or used poor judgment at the time of purchase. Most relationships, entered into with good faith and lived with generous responsibility, shouldn't be considered failures if they are not life-long.

A cartoon in *The New Yorker,* meant to be cynical, shows a rather smug, middle-aged man, saying, "I've been very fortunate. I've liked all my wives." But a great many people who have had more than one important relationship in their lives are similarly fortunate. Helen liked her husband of sixteen years, most of them good and growing years for them both. I liked the woman I lived with before I lived with Helen and am still nourished by those years.

If either Helen or I had said to the other, when we met in New England in 1954, "In 1983, we'll be living on a small island off the coast of British Columbia," the relationship would have staggered to an incredulous halt. For most of us, if we could see into the future, we'd be unable to understand and, therefore, accept it. Yet other people are often more than willing to do it for us.

My silent parents, the mortgage man, our friends all read disaster in the future Helen and I (less courageously) were choosing. Of course, doom and gloom are also predicted for some men and women as they risk commitment, but they don't face the nearly universal discouragement offered to gay and lesbian couples.

I am often asked, mostly by younger women, why it seems so hard for lesbian relationships to last. Accepting responsibility even for oneself can be difficult. How many young people are there around who have learned to love their own lives? Sharing a life doesn't mean that someone else is going to love your life for you but that your own confidence must increase to love another life as well. When everyone around you expects you to fail, it seems the easier if more painful thing to do, before too much is invested, before there is too much to lose.

If a relationship is given its natural life—and no one can predict the length of that—and if there comes a time to move on, there may be hard work in the move, even some regret, but there is neither real loss nor failure. What has been experienced and learned moves with you as surely as the furniture.

Relationships fail only when they are not wholeheartedly entered into, when they are hedged round with reservations, doubts, fears. All our relationships are hedged round with other people's reservations; so it is the more important for those of us who don't want to live alone to have whole hearts to offer, to have both courage and hope that we'll be delighted to be where we are thirty years from now, even if it happens to be on a little island out in the drink with walking canes at the back door.

The Last To Know

Sometimes I think parents should be the last to know. Too often, if they come upon the evidence themselves by reading their children's mail or discovering them in bed with lovers, they react with punitive swiftness which even they come to regret, whether they've seen a lover jailed or confined their offspring to mental hospitals. That sort of thing is still going on.

Unless you are fortunate enough to come out in a supportive and proud gay community, your first experiences of your own sexuality may be negative or at best ambivalent. Your temptation to tell your parents is to shift the blame to them. Usually they are all too willing to feel even guiltier than you do. But they can respond very much as you have, trying to toss that burning shame back on you with such unattractive outcries as (from Father) "I don't need to hear that crock of shit!" and (from Mother) "I'll die of shame" before they fall to blaming each other: "I told you to get his hair cut before he was twenty-one," and "If you hadn't ogled her friends as well as mine, she might have liked men."

They are not exactly what you need at that point in your uncertainty about yourself.

If you are going to tell your parents that you're gay, tell them when they need to know, which is usually long after you are first tempted. Some parents can know and not want to know for years.

Most of us, who have not been initially reckless, begin by dropping hints.

Of an aunt you know is gay to her eyebrows, you say, "Do you think Aunt Ettie is a lesbian?"

"Heavens no," your mother answers. "Whatever gave you an idea like that? Her fiance was killed in the war."

Or you lend her a really good gay novel, and she says, "It's well enough written, but I don't like reading about people like that."

If at that point you lose your patience and say bluntly, "Mother, I'm gay," she'll probably retort, "Well, I wouldn't know it from the expression on your face."

Recently I heard about a classic case of avoidance.

Mother: "I suppose you and Sara are like those people in San Francisco."
Daughter: "Well, in fact, yes, Mother, we are."
Mother: "Good, because your father and I never approved of things like that."
Daughter: "But I said, yes, I was like that."
Mother: "Oh well, you'd say anything, wouldn't you?"

Anyone who would push that conversation further is tone deaf.

Parents' acceptance of a child's homosexuality is often a very slow process.

One young man ordered home to Toronto with his lover for a family wedding was told, "For this week I want you both to be heterosexual."

"No way," the young man protested. "We're all the way out of the closet, and we're not going back in."

"Well, you may be out," his mother replied, "but I'm not."

So he and his lover dutifully wore their pink triangles on their undershirts and kissed the bride instead of the groom.

It's not a cop out. Their generosity to the rituals of her world will make it easier for her to grow in generosity toward the rituals of theirs. Parents who are making a real effort to understand are potential allies of great importance to our community. Their coming out is a political act of as great a force as our own, and they don't have the support group we do unless we provide it for them.

That classically angry graffiti scrawled across a wall, "My mother made me a homosexual," was lovingly answered with "If I gave her some yarn, would she make me one, too?"

Not until you are as confident of your desire as that, as ready to celebrate your own erotic joy, are you ready to tell your parents, to teach your parents that your sexuality is not a matter about which anyone need feel guilty. Their bigotry, like your own, is founded in ignorance and fear, and it is overcome, as your own has been, by love, not only theirs for you, but even more importantly yours for them.

It is by our love, and only by our love, that we can require our parents to be as shameless and proud as we are.

I've seen buttons recently which say, "Have you hugged your mother today?" and "Have you hugged your father today?" Maybe soon there will be buttons which say, "Have you hugged your daughter today?" and "Have you hugged your son today?" If we have to let our parents be the last to know, they may be among the first to understand that "flaunting it" is what love is all about, in all its manifestations.

Border Crossings

At U.S. Customs in the Vancouver Airport, Helen Sonthoff and I stood waiting to have our holiday luggage checked through for our annual trip to the desert. The customs officer was in a bad mood, a signal for me to be wary and polite, the more so because Helen is inclined instead to respond to rudeness with something like, "Young man, you are a *civil* (pause) *servant,*" while an imaginary cell door closes in my mind.

Having discovered undeclared cheese in the luggage of the unfortunate fellow ahead of us, the officer's lust for discovery was whetted, and he went through Helen's clothes as if he were washing them by hand. Finding nothing, he took my declaration, stared at it and then tore it up.

"You don't need that. You live at the same address."

So we moved on to immigration with only one declaration. Asked where mine was, I explained what had happened.

"Are you two related then?" the immigration officer asked.

"No," Helen replied cheerfully. "Just *very* good friends."

I felt like a child in the middle of a game: "Take two

giant steps forward and then freeze."

But nothing happened. Helen doesn't read, as I do, the reports of harassment at borders, particularly the American border. She was surprised at my interpretation of events. But she did agree with me that we should avoid being victims of a setup, stay in control, as much as we could, of any scene to be made. If we decide we want to make an issue of being allowed into the States, we'll do it when we've arranged for photographers and reporters to be present.

When we came back into Canada, we went through separately at two different booths.

"Identification please," the Canadian immigration officer said as he looked down at my declaration.

While I searched in my handbag for my passport, I heard him say, "Hey, well, welcome home."

I looked up into his handsome young face and did not recognize him as an ex-student or anyone I'd met at a party.

"I just saw the rushes of your interview down at Gable-vision. They're great! I really wanted to come along on that one, but we were told only the absolute minimum of men could go on that crew."

"I didn't make that stipulation," I said.

"I know. It's just that we're learning to be tactful."

I couldn't quite believe I was having this kind of conversation, even at Canadian immigration.

"Where's Helen?" he asked.

I nodded to the next booth.

"Hi, Helen," he called over. "Hope you had a good trip."

"Who was that?" she asked.

"A gay brother."

"Beautiful Canada!" Helen said. "Isn't it wonderful to be home?"

Last May, when I went to New York by myself to collect an award from The Fund for Human Dignity, I went through American immigration in Calgary, of all places. Another surly fellow shot aggressive questions at me. Where? How long? "Business or pleasure?"

"Business," I said.

"What *kind* of business?"

"I'm a writer," I said. "I'm having lunch with my agent and dinner with the Governor of New York."

"What's his name?" he challenged.

I told him, and as I did, I thought this probably should have been the time because refusing me entry into the country for an event at which the Governor was to be guest speaker would be news, but I had no photographer, no reporter, and it was costing the Fund a thousand dollars to get me there. I got back on the plane and only made political use of my experience by tattling on that immigration officer to the Governor and assembled audience.

I came back into Canada by way of Toronto where a very regulation-loving young woman asked what I had.

"A plaque," I said. I couldn't bring myself to admit that I also had a soap dish in the form of an old fashioned bathtub from the Plaza Hotel, a legal souvenir.

"How much is it worth?"

"I have no idea."

"Take it to the appraiser's desk over there."

For the first time, I was glad I had a four-hour layover. Again I had to admit that I really did have no idea of the plaque's value.

"Let me see it," the young man said. "No idea at all?"

"None," I said. "I'm sure I couldn't sell it."

He paused to read what was written on it: "The Fund for Human Dignity Award of Merit is presented to Jane Rule for her contribution to the education of the American Public about the lives of Lesbians and Gay Men, May 16, 1983."

"An ambition rather than an accomplishment, I'm afraid," I said.

"Anyway, that's a pretty nice thing to have. Must make you feel proud."

"Thank you."

"Let's call it $50." But he didn't fill out any form, just handed it back to me and smiled.

He didn't see the bathtub, whose value I couldn't have reported either. In a $125 room, how much is a courtesy soap dish worth?

I will probably always hope to be treated civilly at the border rather than plan a confrontation. Though I have been so generously honored in the States, it is obvious that lessons, at our borders anyway, are being better learned in Canada.

The Socially Handicapped

The reason the physically and mentally disabled, racial minorities, homosexuals, people with criminal records and women are lumped together is that they are all perceived to be socially handicapped. The difficulty these groups experience in working together is that most don't like to be linked with one or more of the other groups, feel morally diminished and unfairly stigmatized.

The disabled don't want to be associated with criminals and homosexuals who are responsible for their own predicaments. Racial minorities don't want to be considered among people about whom something is wrong, rejecting the implication that there is anything wrong with not being white. Homosexuals are leery of any suggestion that they might be either sick or criminal. Those with criminal records want those records canceled when their prison terms have been served rather than their being made into a special category of people. Women, who are the majority, find their presence on the list of socially handicapped untenable.

Each objection is understandable. Our own baggage of unacceptability is cumbersome enough without being weighed down with problems which are not only not ours but seem to us to cloud issues central to us. Each group also seems to itself, in one way or another, a little more socially acceptable than the others. It is particularly confusing for those of us who fit into more than one of the categories with each of them competing for our allegiance even to the point of denying the others. The values of each group often conflict with the values of the others.

Denying our common predicament is a defense which will keep us locked inside our minority view of ourselves. We are together for better protection under the law. Even more important than practical politics is what this stand does to change our perception of ourselves in relationship to our culture. When we really see that the vast majority of people are perceived to be socially handicapped, in need of special legislation to guarantee our rights against the prejudices we suffer from, we are in a position to question sharply the values of the culture itself and our own need to be acceptable in its terms.

Who is acceptable in this society? The white, bright, rich, whole heterosexual male. And the white, rich, whole heterosexual female if attached to such a male. I know enough of these to be sure in my own mind that their values are not mine, that their judgments of me are, therefore, irrelevant to me. I have no investment at all in being acceptable to them. I can be accepting of them only as they individually reject their privilege and work for the civil rights of all people.

The approval we crave as social animals has finally to be outgrown so that we can take charge of our lives, come to our own terms, for anyone who doesn't is truly handicapped, deluded into believing that the rewards are worth the brutalizing conformity. Some of the saddest people I know were the silverware ads of my generation, for their "success" has made them no less vulnerable to despair, and the more bitterly surprised for all they were promised.

Those of us who, for whatever reasons, have had to make

what we could out of what the world calls a bad hand may not, in fact, have had such bad cards to play after all if they've made us revalue and redesign the game. If we have any sense, we learn to make and keep our own promises to ourselves and become accepting rather than accepted people. None of us should have trouble identifying with the physically and mentally disabled, colored, gay, criminal, female population. We are victims of nothing but a social brutality we can change, for together we are the people the government can be called upon to serve, not in token gestures here and there, a minor land claim settlement, one government building with wheelchair access, one sheltered workshop, one city's fair housing and employment bylaw, sops to each of our fragments. Together we can demand justice and get it.

The Myth of Genital Jealousy

Sexual fidelity is the most misunderstood, overburdened and abused of our so-called principles. It is based not on a concept of love but on a concept of property. Though the church has required men as well as women to mouth such phrases as "forsaking all others," sexual fidelity for men has only recently become anything but a joke. That is, a woman can now make property claims as a result of a man's infidelity. But basically sexual fidelity had been the method by which a man ensured that he was not getting used goods and that his wife's children would be his own, entitled to inherit his property.

In relationships which are formed without motives of protecting property or progeny, based on attraction and companionability, why is sexual fidelity an issue at all? Why can't it be settled easily, without argument, as irrelevant? For surely, if relationships are based on love, the possessiveness and deprivation inherent in sexual fidelity are alien to it.

Two lines of argument stand against that simplicity. One is that sexual fidelity has become an important metaphor for loyalty and trust in relationship. The other is that sexual jealousy is fundamental to human passion, and any behavior that encourages it will eventually destroy love.

There is no reason why two people shouldn't between themselves choose sexual fidelity as an expression of loyalty and trust, but sexual fidelity of itself has nothing to do with loyalty and trust. How often does the faithful wife mock her husband's taste and judgment as party entertainment and fiddle the bills to spend money without his approval? How often do faithful lovers of any sort belittle each other and lie to each other as negative ways to express their freedom from each other? For most human beings grow restless in sexual prisons, increasingly bewildered by the negativity of what is called love.

Jealousy is common if not fundamental in human feeling. Because it is considered inappropriate to be jealous of another person's beauty, intelligence, luck or wealth, sexual jealousy becomes the only acceptable outlet for our insecurities. It is not all right to envy your lover's good job, talent for falling asleep, naturally curly hair, sympathetic mother, but you can let go all that hard, grown-up discipline and have an insane fit over the slightest erotic pleasure he or she takes outside your company. You can act out all your fears of being betrayed and prove just what a passionately loving person you are all at the same time. And in the early stages of a relationship, the "erring" lover can take some sheepish pride at inspiring such outbursts. My landlady once poked another woman in the eye and then announced, "I just saved my marriage," while her husband stood admiringly by.

At issue really is not sex at all, which can be as casual as a game of tennis, as friendly as a long correspondence, as important as one of the languages of a lifelong living with. There isn't any real reason why we should be forced to choose only one among those experiences. If we could get free of the narrow moral judgment that makes sexual behavior the dumping ground for childish insecurities, we would be able to design a marvelous variety of relationships to suit the variety of people we are. We have to begin not only by lying less but by telling the truth more.

I suspect that fidelity like celibacy is the free choice of only a few as a lifelong commitment. We are, most of us, various in our sexual interests. We are influenced by health, work, other people's needs as well as our own in what we choose to do or not to do.

I read just the other day that among lesbians monogamy is at the moment politically correct. I not only want the church and state out of the bedrooms of the nation; I want the lesbian, gay and women's movements out of mine and yours.

I care very much about loyalty and trust, about involvement that lasts and grows, about harmony and about joy. Sex is only one of the various languages in which to express those values and is not the basis of any of them. Love is. It can be celibate, monogamous, multifarious. But it cannot be bought, insured, taxed or sold. We are not each other's property, in bed or out of it. The children gay people cherish are mostly not our own. What we could leave them is the knowledge that they are not sexual "things," owned and bartered, but people, free to love as they can find out how.

The Question of Children

It is fashionable in some circles to speak of children as the blight of the heterosexual world, burdening those of more enlightened sexuality with noise pollution, road hazards, and school taxes. One of the "benefits" of a gay retirement home is that one wouldn't have to sit in a rocking chair next to someone with a wallet full of pictures of grandchildren. Having visited several retirement compounds on the southern desert, I've noticed that even heterosexuals in no small numbers want to escape the sound, sight and cost of children.

Barbara From said to me defensively, "I suppose you think having children is an ego trip." Quite the opposite. Now that children are not needed as unpaid farm workers and cannot be sent out at six or seven to work in factories and mines, now that birth control gives people some choice, children are neither necessary nor inevitable. They are, instead, a luxury which some can ill afford and others simply don't want. Abortion is more often the answer to those women who try the pregnancy route to marriage.

Yet, as a gay life style becomes increasingly an open

option for people, those who at first conformed to heterosexual expectations bring children with them into their
new lives. And custody cases are being won now by gay
parents who insist that their obligation to and love for their
children is in no way altered by their claiming of their own
sexuality.

Some lesbians are arranging pregnancy by otherwise un-
interested men or sperm banks. I have talked with men who
would like to adopt children.

I suspect a disproportionate number of us work with
children as educators, social workers, nurses and doctors.
And many of us who don't have children participate in the
raising of our nieces and nephews and our friends' children.
A friend of ours with a six-week-old baby phoned at mid-
night and said, "You like this kid, don't you?" We agreed
that we did. "Well then, come and get him before we kill
him."

The difficulty of combating the notion that all of us
dislike children is the conflicting but even more deeply held
conviction that we seduce children. Most of us who have
or work with children feel we have to stay in the closet in
order to be allowed to continue to care for them.

Yet, as in every other area where we are working for our
rights, only visibility will bring about change. The twenty
or so children who use our pool every afternoon from 3 to
5 will have a harder time growing up fearful and bigoted
about lesbians, and their parents are being educated at the
same time. When a couple of the little girls announced that
when they grew up they were going to live together like
Helen and me, there was no parental outcry.

Before we settle for being the smug answer to the population explosion, let us acknowledge that we have parents
among us, that many of us have a sensibility which makes us
particularly good with children, being less apt to make rigid
role requirements, more sensitive to their bewilderments and
need for reassurance, able to establish relationships with
them that don't have to be rebelled against because we know,

at first hand, the value of accepting difference and are not allowed to forget it.

The only love in which possessiveness is generally frowned on is that of adults for children. We learn to take responsibility for their safety, well being, and education whether they are ours or not, even without knowing them. Far from being an experience to avoid, it is the model for the concern we might feel for adults as well.

I don't mind looking at pictures of other people's grand-children, but I hope where I am I'll see the kids themselves.

Integration

I try not to make a principle of being politically incorrect, for rebelling against a code can be as limiting as serving it. I depart, valuing the journey.

I object to lesbian separatism because it, like all forms of bigotry, judges people by gender and class rather than as individuals. To assume that all the negative traits we call male would disappear if there were no men is to reveal the basic error of labeling aggression, competitiveness, and violence masculine. The Margaret Thatchers and Indira Ghandis and Golda Meirs of this world should disabuse us of the hope that women, given power, would necessarily run a more peaceful world than men. Finally, lesbian separation would not simply cut women off from men, but cut lesbians off from the majority of women who will not be persuaded that isolation from men can solve anything.

I do, however, support the right of any beleaguered group to have opportunities to be exclusive. In the early days of the women's movement, I saw how badly inhibited women could be by the mere presence of a man without reference to his behavior. Heterosexual women particularly seemed to feel it impossible to be outspoken and frank. It is not the lesbian separatists in the women's movement who have kept it generally exclusive but the majority of heterosexual women who need a great deal more experience of being autonomous individuals before they have the confidence to cope with mixed groups.

But exclusiveness must be a stage in development, not a goal. A group of people who have suffered as much as women—and particularly lesbians—from being excluded can seize separation as a right for themselves only in revenge. We have instead to learn to overcome our passive education and continue to insist on taking up the duties and privileges that should belong to every individual. In short, we have to teach men to stop being separatists, not embrace their mistake for ourselves.

The argument that men will never voluntarily give up the power they have is convincing only when the political solution is "giving up" rather than "sharing." Though there is real hostility between men and women in the gay community, there is a growing concern among the men anyway to change that attitude as part of changing the whole climate in which they live. That lesbians refuse to participate where they are given second-class citizenship is important. Where they refuse to cooperate with gay men simply because they are men is finally self-defeating. Science fiction utopias are escape literature, not maps of the future which, if it arrives, will be as real as the present, in which we should each be aware that we need all the help we can get.

Only a few years ago Vancouver pubs were segregated, "Men Only" and "Ladies and Escorts." What a hullabaloo there was on the waterfront when the barriers came down, and women could get into the men's section on Friday nights to rescue some part of the week's pay. Well, until women are paid as well as men and the care of children is shared, men will have to put up with that. And I'd, meanwhile, like to push forward against male separatism elsewhere.

Integrated toilets in office buildings would break up the unofficial committee meetings where so many of the real decisions are made. (Sorry, fellas, but there must be some other place you could meet for more personal matters.) Once that's done, who knows? We might even have business lunches together. And, for good or ill, we'd learn that the failings of our world are human, rather than male or female, as are our strengths. Instead of endlessly passing the buck between the sexes, we might come to understand that we lost our innocence together because we wanted to know, and only together have we a chance to use that knowledge with integrity, some as lovers, all as friends and equals.

I wonder how the moral climate of the world would have been changed if Cain and Abel had been, instead of brothers, brother and sister, if incest instead of murder had been one of our founding truths. But we can make new myths for love between brothers, between sisters, and give the lie to that old murderous necessity. We must.

Drag

I wasn't one of those kids who tried to dress the cat in baby clothes. Even with my dolls I was more apt to operate on them than dress them up. Until I actually had my tonsils out, I would have said I'd rather do that than go shopping. I didn't look at what I tried on; I felt it, finger prying at a tight sleeve or discovering an itch against wool, stomach out against a tight saddle. I did look at my feet in the small x-ray machines which used to be standard equipment in shoe stores and felt pity for those bones, pinched and painful there in the dark. My only requirement for clothes was that they cause as little pain as possible.

Yet at twelve I gave in to being strung up like a puppet in a garter belt, bandaged by a bra, hoisted to 6'3" on high heels, mouth bloodied with lipstick, earlobes throbbing with pearls. I didn't have to wear nail polish because my father said it made a woman look as if she'd just devoured her young. Fortunately, eye makeup was not yet popular. I could still rub my eyes.

For twenty years I went around looking like that, even when I was at home if I was expecting guests. Then after a long flight back from Europe, in an elegant navy suit, no more designed for standing in than for sleeping in, on 2½" heels, my face unwashed but newly encrusted with make-up, I waited in Kennedy Airport to claim two forty-pound air trunks from a moving belt about five feet off the ground. A 6'5" uniformed attendant watched me swing those manuscript and book-laden backbreakers onto a cart and said, "Well, how does it feel to be liberated?" I was too angry to reply, "Welcome to the land of eunuchs in uniform."

When I got home, I threw out every pair of heels I had. It took me a bit longer to get rid of all the skirts, but, since pant suits had begun to be popular, I decided to be a trend-setter in wearing them even for teaching and going out to dinner. Very few women of my generation gave up make-up when the kids did, feeling too exposed without it. I had always felt exposed by it, leaving marks of my oral obsessions on cigarette butts, empty glasses, napkins, other people's clothing and faces.

For the past twenty years the only skirts I have worn are tents made out of brightly patterned, no-iron sheets for me by my sister because I don't have to wear shoes with them, and nightgowns since I don't wear shoes to bed.

I do dress up, rarely to please myself, usually simply to indicate that I respect special occasions, a dinner party, a concert. My parents have designed and made for me a collection of beautiful needlepoint vests. Over a black shirt and black trousers, they can take me anywhere on flat, black shoes. They pack well. They are comfortable enough to sleep in if I have to. They don't attract hostile attention.

I have found it hard to understand why men, born to be free of all that physical torture, exept perhaps for a collar and tie, are ever tempted to take on the masochism of women's dress and make-up. Surely they can't envy us all that mess as well as discomfort. If, as has been suggested, they really envy the birds and want male plumage of their own, there are more comfortable ways of being flamboyant.

Does wanting to be more seductive, more yielding

somehow require a garter belt and a bra, high heels and stockings? Wigs except in snow storms are hot and itchy.

Or is it because women's clothes are forbidden to men as men's aren't to women, that part of the attraction is the danger of it? I'm not getting away with anything if I go to the corner store in men's cords, sneakers and a velour shirt. A man in a woman's dress would cause alarm.

I don't have the difficulty some women do who see men in drag as a way of mocking women. There is something inherently silly about all seductiveness. There's nothing wrong with being silly occasionally, even if it underlines the silliness of other people's behavior. It took a uniformed eunuch to mock me into sanity.

Perhaps men dress up like women to please other men, just as women do. If men really are turned on by all that awful underwear, leg and footwear, all that paint and headachy perfume, then maybe they should have been wearing it all along. We should see our drag queens as the great liberators of women, relieving us of all that seductive pain which has so little to do with our own pleasure. We should encourage panty raids and thefts of bras off clotheslines. If what men want is our underwear, let them be welcome to it. It's a great swap for the shirts off their backs which we wear so comfortably.

I have been considering a tuxedo, but the starched shirt front puts me off, and I don't really like ties. Are there decent pockets in the trousers? It can't be as much of a drag as a gown, but it might make me too formidable. I can't wear anything that precludes me from going into my big, dumb, gentle animal act, by which I don't so much want to seduce the world as make it a kinder, more tolerant place to live.

Asking for the Moon

Lillian Faderman in *Surpassing the Love of Men,
Romantic Friendships and Love Between Women from the
Renaissance to the Present* began her study to find the
answer to a puzzling question, why passionate relationships
between women have been condoned in other eras and per-
secuted in our own. She marks the change in attitude at
World War I. In her long, fascinating and detailed study,
she comes to several related conclusions. The first is that,
since women were conditioned to deny their own sexual
appetites, the vast majority of relationships between women
before the 20th century, however passionate in language,
were not overtly sexual. The second is that, though many
women longed to live together, only a rare few had the
economic independence to act on such a choice. Only when
women began to achieve some degree of independence did
their relationships with other women become a threat to
men. What had been viewed as harmless, even charming,
now had to be labeled immoral and sick. It is always difficult for me to accept how much of our behavior is conditioned, how bound we are within the ignorance of our

time, but the more I read of Lillian Faderman, the more convinced I became that women's knowledge of their own sexuality in western culture, anyway, is a development of the 20th century.

If the vast majority of women, until very recently, lived their lives without sexual pleasure, believing with men that such an appetite was exclusively male, we are now not simply in the business of breaking the silence about sexual experience but actually experiencing female sexuality for the first time. If the female orgasm is no older than, let's say, the airplane, it is a revolutionary discovery of basic importance to women, or could it instead be a gigantic fad like jogging from which the majority will withdraw, finding it too much work, dangerous to health, unnecessarily complicating and time-consuming for the actual value of it? Will people look back at this period of sexual liberation with a sense of disbelief that I have in thinking about the probable innocence of sexual pleasure in my grandmothers? I know it sounds preposterous that women might, in fact, withdraw from their own new understanding of their bodies, but the implications of sexual pleasure for women haven't yet been evaluated.

There is already a tone of wistfulness in Lillian Faderman about the innocence there once was between women, who now don't have the option of ignoring the sexual implications in their relationships with each other. Oddly it is now easier for a man and woman to claim platonic relationship which involves affection and loyalty than it is for women to be intimate friends without being lovers.

Though there have been attempts by women to make experience as quickly and impersonally available for them as for men, I think it is not simply lack of economic clout or spirit of enterprise that gives us no equivalent to the steam baths. Our most impressive demonstration, the "Take Back the Night" march in San Francisco, was for freedom from sexual molesting on the streets. The growing protest against pornography in the women's movement also seems more important to us than developing a pornography of our own to indulge our newly discovered sexuality.

Whatever knowing that we are capable of sexual pleasure means to us, it obviously doesn't mean what many men hoped it would, our finally agreeing with them that, if rape is inevitable, we should relax and enjoy it. Nor do I think it necessarily means that great numbers of women want their relationships with other women sexually defined.

If we are as human creatures so communally defined that most of us can have been kept in sexual ignorance for centuries, we have to realize how fragile our control is over our knowledge and what we are to do with it. That our sexual appetites are entirely detached from their biological purpose may be more of an evolutionary joke than a blessing, as our walking upright is often suggested to be. Certainly both can be hard on the back, but our brains, about which we are so proud, may give us at least a sense of irony about our condition.

Our new freedom is as susceptible to new bondage as our ignorance has been in the past. What we are capable of is not necessarily what should define our choices. Reaching the moon has, for instance, proved a very expensive and sterile experience, given what we might have done with all that money, intelligence, and courage. In the discovery of the multiple orgasm, it's not really a question of how many we can have but how many we want, with whom, if at all. In order to answer that question fairly for each woman, of the sexual options now being offered to women, there must be the freedom to choose, "None of the above." To proceed more cautiously, to integrate our sexuality with all the other aims and privileges of our lives may save us, and men with us, from the mindless brutality male pornography promises in the name of sexual freedom. We may have been slow to evolve our awareness of our own sexual pleasure not only because we have been perceived as the property of men but because it is only really awakened in a climate of tenderness and equality, the experience of rare women in the past. The erotic democracy we dream toward may require a quality of innocence, of altruism only our grandmothers can teach us, however new the forms.

Home and Mother

I have met a few lesbian couples who have lived together for years without sexual connection, one maintaining near celibacy, the other leading an active sexual life elsewhere. I have encountered this model of Victorian marriage more often between men. The older they are, the more this fact about their relationship is kept a guilty secret. Younger people are apt to talk about the convenience rather than the commitment of being "just friends." Though increasing numbers of people reject the ideal, that one-flesh-faithful-unto-death still haunts us, making what we think of as more rational arrangements still dubious and guilt-ridden.

Is celibacy in a long term relationship an attempt at a different sort of fidelity, removed from sexuality which, if combined with love, so often produces those monstrous children, possessiveness and jealousy? Remove sex from a relationship, and there may be freedom to enjoy commitments less likely to pall of work, hobbies, house and garden, friends, animals. That is often the explanation after the fact, but it is not usually on those terms such a relationship begins.

Romantic love offers no model for passionate peers. Most men fall in love with women, after all. Those who are attracted to other men, if they are to follow the romantic model, must assert their superiority or relinquish it. Auden and Forster, for example, both chose men much younger than themselves, less competent or inferior in social status, in need of protection and support. Auden's lover rejected the role of inferior finally by rejecting Auden sexually. As often, the rejection comes from the man who has perceived himself the superior. Once he recognizes his lover as a friend and peer, he can no longer see him as an object of passion. Sexual attraction depends on both partners accepting basic inequality.

Inequality in casual relationships, where love is not an issue, may seem more tolerable. So, just like the Victorian husband made to feel ashamed of his sexual needs, the homosexual spares his partner the humiliation of his appetite and takes it instead to the bars, parks, and baths. Sex is sport, recreation, which has nothing to do with the center of living, home.

But there has to be a center, one who rarely strays, for the relationship to continue. Of those men who accept the role of tender of the hearth, it has been recently said, "They need women's liberation more than most women do." For, like women, they are expected to nurse and comfort those home from the game with bruised egos and hepatitis. Alas, without sex there can still be jealousy, and the contemptuous bitchery directed at young punks and tricks again sounds very much like the Victorian wife on the subject of prostitution.

The lesbian pattern of celibacy within a relationship seems more often to come from guilt about all sexual experience which in one may result in rejection of the body, in the other a "sinning" and "being forgiven," virgin mother and child into old age.

It may be that the homosexual community is taking longer to emerge from Victorian attitudes toward sex, having suffered a great deal more from hostile disapproval of its appetites. As people with growing self-respect and deepening self-knowledge, we mustn't go on imitating heterosexual models which don't suit heterosexuals all that often and certainly have little relevance for us.

It may also be more difficult for men than for women who have the support of the women's movement in radically changing their ways of living. I hear far more genuine questioning among women, far more fierce defending among men, whether of bars and parks or sex with children if I'm listening to homosexuals, of patriarchal privilege among my heterosexual male friends: "Well, maybe I just want to be an old fart: it's my house!"

Every choice in a relationship has obvious limitations. We are not all alike in our needs and aspirations. A nun friend explains, "Celibacy is the only way I can manage loving so many people. Otherwise it would be far too complicated." "Give me the complications!" retorts one of my young, experimenting friends. "But sometimes I feel," says a recently divorced woman trying to figure out her new life, "as if I'm using everyone." If we dared to use each other for real understanding of our experience, our sexual daring might be less compartmentalized, defensive, and guilty.

Lesbian Leadership

A young black lesbian named Evelyn White came to interview me for a gay paper published in Seattle. "Do you think of yourself as a Canadian?" she asked. "Yes," I said. "But you were American." "Yes." "That's what makes it hard for us. We know you were an American, but you are a Canadian, and that means we should be polite to you." "Why?" "Well, that makes you a foreigner, and we shouldn't trash foreigners." "Why would you want to trash me?" "Because we think of you as a leader." "And you trash leaders?" "Of course."

Out of that exchange came two questions for me. The first has to do with why writers particularly have been singled out as leaders by both the women's movement and the lesbian community. Writers are certainly not the political leaders and role models for society at large. Norman Mailer may have run for the office of mayor of New York City, but he wasn't elected. Nor are writers the leaders of other minority groups. In the black community, in the Jewish community, they are the rebels, much more often shaming their communities with their own foibles than inspiring them with new pride and political direction.

It has been suggested to me that women look to writers as leaders because they break the silence women have felt imprisoned in. Tilly Olsen has written about what silences us, the burdens of housework, children, wage earning, all undermining the development of and confidence in one's own voice. Kate Millett has written of the rampant misogyny that informs our most honored literature and degrades us. If such insight opens the doors of the prison, shouldn't those writers also lead the way into freedom? It has been suggested to me that lesbians have felt not only silenced but invisible. By writing about lesbian experience, by accepting the public definition of lesbian, I and other writers like me have created a new visibility. Then shouldn't it also be our job to show lesbians how to be visible?

The media must take a lot of the blame for the hideous distortion of our visibility, Kate Millett painted like a thug on the cover of *Time Magazine*, but the record crowds who came out to hear her speak were women. Increasingly, she didn't say what they wanted to hear. She said she was in pain. She said her life was being taken out of her hands. She said she was being eaten alive. Sometimes she did nothing but read from a new manuscript, as if she were like any other writer asked to perform. Her audiences, who had not come to hear her as a writer but as a lesbian and a leader, cheated of inspiration trashed her. Yet what else could they have expected of her? She never claimed to have a platform; she hadn't stood for election; she wasn't a leader. The pattern has been similar for other writers. Rita Mae Brown's audiences tell her she spends too much money on clothes and cars, is elitist and sometimes closeted in her affairs; and she tells them she doesn't want any downwardly mobile among the middle class telling her who was raised poor and has earned her own money how to spend it. Her last novel, prefaced with a statement that anyone who doesn't like it can write one of her own, deals with every known deviant behavior except lesbianism. One partner of an apparently lesbian couple turns out to be male.

In fact, most writers identified with women's or lesbian causes behave like writers, not like leaders. They insist on their autonomy, their right to say and do anything they please, even if it is to write about or be the Empress without her clothes. Bad at kissing babies, shaking hands, bad at all the daily political housework leaders are supposd to concern themselves with, they are either drunken cavorters on the stage or recluses as writers have always been.

In every consciousness-raising group I've sat in, it is not politically correct to have a leader. In one we all sat on the floor because there weren't enough chairs to go round. Though such insistences on equality can be uncomfortably leveling, the symbol is an important one. We gather to share our experiences and ideas, to sit at no one's feet.

My second question, therefore, is not about our misuse of writers as leaders but why we are looking for leaders at all, outside and against the political climate we are trying to create among ourselves. The answer I am given is that role models are necessary if we are to change our lives.

Maybe it's a failure of my temperament, but the only role models I ever used were people who failed at everything I thought important. They functioned as cautionary tales rather than inspirations, and I can still occasionally check myself out against them, particularly as I monitor my relationships with the young and my behavior in the public world. Nobody needs to look far for people like that. They are all around us. Our pilgrims' progress is to get around their self-pity and vanity on our own particular journeys which, for an unbeliever like me, can't be defined by God or man or even other women.

When I agree to do one of those ridiculous interviews for magazines like *The Canadian* or *Today*, I am ostensibly asked because I am a writer seeking publicity for my books. I know I am really being interviewed because I am a lesbian, a far more titillating title than novelist. Since the interviewer is setting out to use me, I have no qualms about using the interview to make educational points, not for the women's or lesbian communities who know perfectly well that lesbians can live quite ordinarily in the world but for the hetero-sexual community too long willfully ignorant of us as people. If I can persuade the interviewer to present me to that public as an amused, tolerant, moderately successful woman living without discomfort in a small community, no matter how simple-minded or silly the article, a point has been made.

I am not, as a result of such activities any more than as a writer, setting myself up as a leader or role model for anyone. If my community, egged on by the media, tries to turn me into one, I will fail just as others have failed before me not simply because I am a writer but because leaders of that sort are damaging to the sense of self-worth and self-direction all women's consciousness raising is about. The political work we have to do has no room for the power of office, the idealizing of authority, hero worship. Only when we've got rid of all that claptrap, so much energy spent in raising up what then must inevitably be torn down, will we be free to get on with the real job of recognizing each other's strengths, our strength together to change the climate of the world we live in.

The real power of books is their deep companionability. We learn from them as we learn from the deep companion-ability of love to know our own hearts and minds better. As lesbians we should know we no more want to be led by the nose by our writers than we do by our lovers, but to be together equally in each other's presence.

The Affirmative Action Novel

Sometimes, after reading particularly silly reviews, I speculate on the possibilities of an affirmative action novel with fair employment for all minorities. In order not to be accused of tokenism, I would have to create a cast of thousands because no self-respecting blind person would feel fairly represented by, say, a woman with one arm, and someone dying of cancer won't readily identify with a diabetic. A native Indian does not see her plight in the circumstance of a Canadian-born Japanese, and a black from Barbados is not a black from Detroit or Nova Scotia.

I suddenly remember sitting in my brother's office while he called the employment office to find a secretary for his small California firm, "Send me a black, crippled, lesbian with a Spanish surname," he said gloomily. "That's the only way I can get enough brownie points for federal contracts."

That may be a solution to his problem, but, if I started to burden my characters with at least four minority claims apiece, I'd straight off be accused of creating grotesques, making fun of the lot of us. Whether or not in real life we sometimes lack dignity (I think of the beautiful Robert Creeley, put in a back brace in his teens; when his glass eye fell out, he was unable to bend over and pick it up, the reason he gave up wearing the eye), an author has to respect her characters and not play god to a cast of Jobs.

The trouble, too, with this impossibly large group of characters, some with diseases I can't even spell, some with ethnic backgrounds I'd need years to research, some with sexual preferences before which my imagination fails, is that they wouldn't get along very well together, ghettoized and elitist as most of them would be. Remember those scenes on the national news a few months ago, two groups of people both denouncing violence against minorities, beating each other over the head with their placards in Stanley Park? When I was young, I ran a recreation program at a receiving centre for orphans in London. When I tried to organize team sports, the kids stole the shoes of their own teammates. Even in a dart game, they preferred moving objects to the board. But, if I'm trying to keep out of political trouble, I can't very well portray the lack of sympathy any self-respecting minority has for any other, never mind those in our own ranks. Only the small "l" liberal white can be guilt-tripped into "identifying with others," and she certainly has no place in such a book.

We are at our least tolerant when we are working for our own minorities, passionate and partisan for our own cause, thinking it can be emblematic of all struggles in an unjust world. The political animal in each of us is competitive, egotistical, and self-righteous. Even as altruists, we argue for the rights of our starving million against the rights of your starving million. I spent a whole evening defending my contribution to Foster Parents' Plan against demands that I give everything to Tibetan refugees. I would not like to count the number of times I've had to defend myself for writing for *The Body Politic* against the view that I should spend all my time on women's publications.

Actually, the only way I can arrange for characters to

get along relatively well in a book is to show them often ignoring the minorities they belong to, being distracted from the politics they espouse, being particular people on a particular day, going about their domestic, mortal business with its possibilities for humor and tenderness. Crowd scenes tend to violence.

I heard today on the radio that a very successful writer of historical romances was offering, at the price of a little over one hundred thousand dollars, to put anyone into a novel set in the period of her choice. A Texas department store is advertising the project in its Christmas catalogue. Wanting to minorities of your choice in the political climate of your choice is simply an extension of that very expensive and silly fantasy, unless, of course, you are able to write it yourself. I give you only this bit of advice: political writers often find it easier to write about rabbits or Martians than about people. That's because, to the untutored eye, they all look alike.

Straights, Come Out

When I encounter violent homophobia in strangers, I don't often stop to consider with any seriousness where that hatefulness comes from. I ship it out of my consciousness with labels like "ignorant" and "bigoted." If that hostility is aimed directly at me rather than offered at random, I add further labels like "sexually fragile" and "ego damaged," which are not insightful so much as dismissive. I am simply and sensibly protecting myself with a more adult version of "Sticks and stones will break my bones, but names will never hurt me" (which I'm not 100% sure is true).

But we are among those minorities who are confronted not only by the hostility of strangers but by the hostility of our friends and relatives. I'll never forget the sense of pure fear I felt at fourteen when a couple of my school friends, staying overnight, began a conversation with, "What would you do if you were in the same room with a lesbian?" "I'd throw up." "I'd die." Nor do I forget my mother's trying to get a male hair dresser fired because he wore makeup.

The people we know, the people with whom we've

formed our deepest bonds are often as irrationally homophobic as the aggressive kids on the street or the self-
righteous "Moral Majority." (How pleased I was to see the
bumper sticker "The 'Moral Majority' is neither.") Some
of them, confronted with the choice between cherishing a
family member or old friend and cherishing their prejudice,
choose very quickly, but for most it is a very long conflict
between love of a person and hatred of an idea.

Some of us choose quickly, too, react violently to the
first criticism, reject family, friends, the whole straight world,
and establish support systems in the gay world to supplant
what has been lost.

Most of us have internalized enough of society's prejudice to begin our coming out with apologies, and we are
patient, perhaps grateful for the first scraps of tolerance,
even if a mother says to a son, "We'll share this secret because it would kill your father," or a sister says to a sister,
"I pity you."

The difficulty is that as our own perception grows, as
we learn not only to accept but to celebrate our lives, such
limited perceptions of us are not only not enough but in-
sulting. We want the people we love in the straight world
to grow with us. Not enough of them do. As long as we
are modestly ashamed and secretive, our families and friends
can go on caring for us charitably without having to alter
their basic values, but, when we begin to live openly and
proudly, we become threatening.

Most of us don't intend to be threatening, at least not
to the people we love. We try to explain what we've come
to understand for ourselves, that we are no more trying
to rub people's noses in our sexuality than a bride and groom
do, than proud young parents do, that affirming ourselves
is as common and healthy an attitude as it is for anyone
else.

Since I have for years devoted part of my career to
being a public voice for educating people about homosexuality, I may more often than most have to confront

my failures with people I go on caring about. And with them, it does matter to me to try to figure out where all that hatefulness is coming from, why love and knowledge combined don't always eradicate it.

All our relationships are complex, jealousy tangling with pride, derailed expectations keeping company with unexpected generosities, ineptitudes coupling with remarkable grace. Sometimes homosexuality is no more than the handiest stick to beat with, on either side of the argument where something quite other may be at stake.

But what is it for some people of genuine good will that makes it so difficult to accept our sexuality? I come increasingly to believe that they haven't accepted their own. We can sometimes forget, working so hard in our own terms, that we have been required to by a society which is not simply homophobic but generally phobic about sexuality.

If straight people have the decency to be modestly ashamed of their own sexual natures, what right have we to be proud of ours? Marriage for them is not a flaunting but a legalizing of their sexuality. They don't think of children as a celebration of their sexuality but as its redeeming result. St. Paul said, "It is better to marry than burn." But in that anti-sexual church, celibacy is still the ideal. Everyone is *supposed* to be ashamed.

This negative morality which pervades our society is the root not only of homophobia but of the punishing violence of much pornography. We won't move freely in the world until all people are required to confront their sexual natures in order to understand, take responsibility for and celebrate them, as we have had to. For no one who is disappointed or ashamed or frightened of his/her own sexuality is going to be easily tolerant of anyone else's.

Anyone who lives in sexual shame with only the cold comfort that it is at least heterosexual is going to be a difficult person to deal with, unlikely to take kindly to advice from a blatant homosexual. What we may need to do is to persuade our liberated straight friends to help. If they would march under their own banner, "Straights for Peace" or "Straights for the Environment," maybe some of their closeted friends would be encouraged to come out, to repudiate the stork, the cabbage patch, and join us in the mortal sexuality that makes us all kin. But even before that happens, we and they live in the often heart-breaking but hopeful knowledge that we love our enemies.

An Act of God

If AIDS is going to be called an Act of God, I want the phrase interpreted as it is in some insurance policies. I collected 100% instead of the usual $50 deductible when my car was damaged by a fire in the engine. For an insurance agent Acts of God relieve the victim of any responsibility and therefore require total compensation. For God is one of those wanton boys Shakespeare told us about who kill us for their sport. His other names are accident, disease, natural disaster, death. We live in a country which aspires to universal health care, which declares disaster areas for victims of earthquake and flood, which maintains rescue crews for people stranded in storms at sea, trapped in wrecked aircraft, lost on a mountain. For anybody.

Yet when something terrible happens, particularly something before which we are helpless, the greatest temptation is to judge the victim. Victims, too, can seek defense against the irrational by looking for something or someone to blame, even themselves; for whatever cold comfort that is, it can seem preferable to facing the fact of random, morally purposeless disaster.

Illness, accident, and death are not punishments for anything but being born. All our defenses, personal and social, are temporary. All that lives dies. Whatever justice and mercy there are are not divine at all but human, and however faulty and frail they are, however finally defeated, they are the only tools we have in the face of crisis.

A morality based on a fear of death is so ridiculous it should be the source of comedy. All sins are mortal. All virtues are, too. Equally are youth and beauty, age and pain. Neither is it true that only the good die young nor that only the wicked are punished. Morality has nothing to do with death. It has to do with living.

"For the love of God," is usually an expression of exasperation, followed by "Can't you see . . . ?" or "Can't you do . . . ?" something that seems perfectly obvious and sensible to anybody. This God is quite a different sort of fellow from the one who killed mostly people praying in a cathedral during that earthquake in Columbia. His other names are right reason, concern, responsibility. He is, in fact, the insurance agency. A friend of mine, skiing on a slope restricted to skiiers, went over an unexpected bluff thinking, "For the love of God, why didn't I renew my health insurance policy?" Hindsight is only twenty-twenty vision when you live to tell the tale.

There is nothing wrong with foresight, as long as you don't believe in it, as long as it doesn't become a moral superstition. There are no odds against dying. You have to have foresight long enough to know that, too. Then it can be useful for us and our community.

All active gay men and lesbians are risk takers, even those in the closet, because we don't have equal protection under the law. It is worthwhile to work for the time when we do. We also have reason to believe that we often don't have equal treatment in medicine. Why are gay men having to pay for shots against hepatitis B? It is important for us to raise such questions, to report doctors who treat us unequally or not at all, to support our own doctors, to put pressure on research funding agencies and to raise funds ourselves so that our needs are not neglected.

When we confront a new threat to us like AIDS, we must not waste time either fearing or loving God, nor must we listen to anyone else doing it for us. It is not difficult to behave responsibly with those already ill. We can insist on the best medical treatment available and learn, those of us who don't know already, how to participate in the life of someone who is dying.

For those who may be in danger, it is more difficult. We haven't much to go on but educated guesses about cause and treatment and mild to wild predictions about the numbers involved. The baths, like swimming pools during polio epidemics, are suspected as places of contagion, and, since they are used by transients as well as residents of any city, they may be, until the disease is better understood, places of high risk. We are all concerned that health authorities might use the excuse of AIDS to close down the baths and must resist those attempts before evidence justifies it. Defiant denial of any risk would be irresponsible.

It has always been true that certain kinds of diseases are more prevalent among certain groups of people. One out of every four women will have breast cancer, and, though the mortality rate isn't nearly as high as it presently is for AIDS, it kills many more women than AIDS will men. Women who have had children are at higher risk. Nowhere have I seen it suggested that women should stop having children. I know one woman who has had two children after having one breast removed.

Cancer of the cervix, on the other hand, is more common among heterosexual women who have had more than one sexual partner, and doctors have frequently blamed women for a disease they might have avoided and made them feel morally responsible for their illness.

Illness is given moral stigma only when it is related to an activity or a group of people disapproved of.

My niece has five stress fractures in one leg from playing

basketball. I wouldn't play. I wouldn't climb a mountain either, try to cross an ocean alone in a small boat, do a lot of other death-defying things so much admired as human achievements, simply for their own sake.

"Why do they do it, these men?" one of Ethel Wilson's female characters asks. "They do it to be uncomfortable, and unlucky and for the greatest fulfillment of their lives."

For some men the baths may be what mountains are for others, worth the risk for the view at the top, both the experience and the freedom it symbolizes as good a thing to die for or of as any. Many more people die of pleasure than is ever reported in the newspapers, even of the sort reserved for procreation. Why should it be less admirable than falling in battle where people are actually trying to kill each other?

It is not the length but the quality of life that matters to me, more easily said now that I am over fifty. But it has always been important to me to write one sentence at a time, to live every day as if it were my last and judge it in those terms, often badly, not because it lacked grand gesture or grand passion but because it failed in the daily virtues of self-discipline, kindness, and laughter. It is love, very ordinary, human love, and not fear, which is the good teacher and the wisest judge.

Censorship

I am against the present laws on censorship as well as the proposed strengthening of those laws which have been in their present state and would be in their "improved" state used against newspapers like *The Body Politic* and literary works more readily than against those perceived as political sellers of pornography. That opinion makes me no less an objector to pornography than those who invite police to press charges or those who take the law into their own hands and firebomb video stores. It does make me a different sort of political animal, against the law and against violence.

The reason the police and the courts are reluctant to act against sellers of pornography is that "dirty" pictures and "dirty" movies are really just an extension of "dirty" jokes with which men have always entertained themselves. As long as women stay where they belong (at home), they are perfectly safe from this form of male hostility, vented in fantasy. The women who insist on working for a living, walking in the public street, and, worst of all, informing themselves about the nature of pornography get what they are asking for from sexual harassment to rape and murder. Pornography is a cautionary tale for women, part of the power structure to keep us in our places.

The Body Politic, on the other hand, in many of its stances clearly challenges the right of the police to entrap, beat up and jail men engaged in consentual sex with other men. In challenging basic attitudes toward sexuality, it threatens the state's power over other men as well as women and children. It is seen as a threat, a political threat to established order. Once the state's position is clear, it's no longer baffling that The Body Politic has been in court for five years over an article granting some possible benefit to sexual relationships between men and boys, while it took the prodding of women's groups with sympathetic men in support to force the B.C. government to act against films depicting, among other things, a woman being killed by an enema, and that case was over in a matter of weeks, the parties found guilty and given minimal fines.

I think one of the basic failures in recent debates in The Body Politic about pornography and censorship is some women's inability to see that censorship won't work and some men's inability to see that pornography is as important an issue as, and separate from, freedom of expression.

If we are not talking about writing laws, defining pornography doesn't pose as serious a problem. We do have different tastes. Maybe some of mine come from my middle class background. (My mother wouldn't think so!) I have no problem with nudity, with representations of the sexual act. I don't like bodies presented without heads, particularly female bodies. The motive may sometimes be the protection of the individual, but the impression is decapitation, and I also happen to be someone who is attracted to people's faces. This is a matter of taste, and I have no trouble in hoping that a magazine like The Body Politic would be aware of my taste, among others, in making visual choices. What I object to is the representing of acts of violence against bodies in the name of sexual freedom. Live rats, guns and hot hair curling irons placed in women's vaginas are not sexual acts, any more than dismemberment and murder are sexual acts. If these were images to be found only in the archives of criminal psychology, women might not be as concerned as they are, but these are the images found in widely circulated films. There are apparently a great many people willing to pay money to look at images of that sort.

I don't find evidence, as some radical feminists do, for the claim that all men are rapists and murderers. If all men are potential rapists and murderers, they are so only as women, too, have a potential for destructuve behavior. We are the same species. Women, however, have been traditionally trained away from destructive behavior (how else would the two-year-olds of the world survive?), except as we can turn it on ourselves in madness and suicide. Why else would Sylvia Plath's suicide inspire any more than pity? Men are trained to kill in circumstances of war. Because for most men such behavior is abhorrent, it must be continually glorified to persuade men against their own moral sense to destroy rather than protect other members of their own species.

We have come to a point in the history of our species where individual and even national survival haven't any meaning. The destructive impulse, therefore, hasn't any claim to social usefulness (if it ever did). If only a very small percentage of the population actually commits suicide or rapes and kills without a specific education to do so, then the educational process which encourages either self-destruction or murder must be reversed, until the chorus, "No, no, we won't go" is universal.

I find the preoccupation with violence in the daily fare on television just as frightening as violent pornography. Hourly men are presented to us as heros who beat up, torture, maim and kill other men. Those victims are "bad guys" who deserve what they get, much as the women in violent pornographic films are presented as beneath contempt. That these are the most common images given to men for their power and self-worth should be as energetically protested by men as by women.

When gay men, in particular, complain about being guilt-tripped by feminists about male aggression, why don't they begin objecting to the monsters made of men in the media? Why don't they begin to boycott the travesty that is made of manhood as women are beginning to make our objections to our being represented as brainless victims not only of men but of personified washing machines and ovens? Mr. Clean isn't even attractive.

It is not only women but men who must stand up and say, "No, that is not who we are." Women, in stating our own case against our misrepresentation in the fantasy life of the world and therefore our lack of representation in the real world sometimes don't want to hear that men are as, if differently, victimized.

This generation of women involved in the feminist movement in Canada are mostly too young to remember world wars. I remember, with horror, the gold stars in windows, marking proudly a house which had lost a son, brother or father. I remember, with horror, a mother proudly receiving her country's honor for having "given" five sons to victory. Whole generations of young men were killed in both those wars. Any woman who proudly sees men off to war has very little moral claim to urge the sanctity of her own life, exempt from the violence she condones.

Men's indifference to pornography as a basic threat to our humane survival is akin to the indifference of men and women alike to the daily glorification of male violence when it is directed against other men, not only in thrillers but on the nightly news where we are supposed to go on applying the brutish morality of "good guys" and "bad guys."

It is not a matter of wanting to turn away from "things unpleasant," from "reality." Both the glory and the terrible vulnerability of human creatures is our ability to learn. The army *can* make a man of you. Marriage *can* make a woman of me. But we do also have some capacity to resist our educations, to influence the world we live in, to change our perceptions of ourselves and other people. If this were not so, those in authority would have no fear of dissenters.

Not so very long ago, children worked in the mines from the age of six, women died young of yearly breeding, and men died exhausted working for their betters. Elsewhere in the world today there is not even that minimal ritual of life in huge refugee populations, in many indigenous populatons. But we do know, because as a culture we have experienced it, that a more humane way to be children and to be men and women is possible.

If we refuse to help create a climate which glorifies mutilation and death, if we protest against it, we can begin to change it. What makes all human atrocities on a large scale possible is the passive acceptance of them by the majority of people who have been conditioned either to feel helpless or to be indifferent to the suffering of others.

Sexual liberation is no more about raping women than it is about bashing queers. Would *The Body Politic* help publicize films that endorsed beating up homosexuals in the park, robbing and murdering them as an acceptable enhancement of manhood, sexually tantalizing? I think not. Yet it has argued that refusing ads from a firm which distributes films abusive to women is an act of negative censorship.

The wide gap between destroying property or calling in the police and helping to sell the stuff offers plenty of comfortable moral and political space to live in. In this consumer society not helping to sell and not buying are very strong weapons in the hands of the people.

Gay men and women can be together on this issue. Women don't have to play into the traps of the moral majority by demanding censorship which will be politically abused. Gay men don't have to condone pornography degrading to women in the name of sexual freedom and freedom of expression. We can together say we don't like it. We won't sell it. We won't buy it. We will instead do everything we can to change the image of man as a defiler of the earth, proving his superiority to nature by destroying it.

The terrifying message of gay liberation is that men are capable of loving their brothers. It should be sweet news to every woman in the world, for, if the capacity of men to love whom they have been taught to treat as competitors and enemies can transcend their education, the world can begin to heal. The message of women's liberation is that women can love each other and ourselves against our degrading education. It is not necessary for men to protect and despise women, nor for women to nurture and fear men. It is time for us to share subversive truths about the courage of men and women to live in diversity and peace.

Sexual Infancy

We have spent too much sexual time either aping hetero-sexual marriage to exonerate ourselves or accepting outlaw status and flaunting it, trying to be either the good or the bad children of our culture. We have not spent enough time defining ourselves, our particular needs, desires, and goals. Every time I try to write about sexual and moral choices, I find myself starting back with Adam and Eve, and I've written the outline of a book rather than an essay before I even get to the 19th century. I feel I have to give historical, scholarly evidence for a view I have arrived at, which is that much of what has been said about human sexuality is so much hocus-pocus, whether it has to do with the evil nature of woman as the downfall of man, the homosexual component in us all which must be sublimated for the sake of human culture, or the dark, anti-social forces in man which make him a rapist and murderer.

We have no real way of knowing what kinds of sexual creatures we would be if we had been allowed to grow up in our sexuality. What we do know is that some of us are so fearful, guilty, and hung up that any sexual experience is too threatening, and many more of us cope only by hedging it round with restrictions and taboos. Those who achieve the freedom to do what they really want often get there only by means of drugs and then feel more comfortable by isolating that experience so that the implications of those appetites don't have to be dealt with in domestic, affectionate living.

We talk too much as if our sexual tastes were fixed. That, too, is a defensive habit of mind. For we all know that we grow and change sexually as we do in every other way, if we allow ourselves to. Edna St. Vincent Millay was my favorite poet and the Catholic spinster school principal an object of my desire when I was fourteen. The first time she ever kissed me was last month when I ran into her visiting another friend in an old people's home. Even she has changed that much! But it's not a fantasy I still cherish. Nor do I any longer read Edna St. Vincent Millay. We grow up. We grow old.

Men, probably because they do not get pregnant, have always been able to confront their sexual needs as something separate from their domestic lives. Men mainly interested in women have had to marry or pay or rape until quite recently. What is remarkable about recreational sex gay men celebrate more and more openly is not its detachment from meaningful relationship—whore houses have provided that for centuries—but its detachment from commerce or coercion. "Instant gratification" is a term associated with infants, something that, as we grow up, we learn not to demand or expect.

What some gay men may always have known is how to recreate their infancy and childhood together. One gay bar in Vancouver is called "The Play Pen." In parks designed for children to play in, in baths like permissive nurseries or playschools, where grownups are there only to help if people hurt themselves and to clean up the mess, polymorphous perversity, that fancy term for being unhousebroken and erotically fixed on everything, can be celebrated.

Gay men have been so busy defending their right to these pleasures against the outrage of the moral majority and police raids that there hasn't been comfortable space, in public anyway, for them to discuss the limitations as well as the pleasures of such sexual activities. Gay men who don't like the parks and baths speak freely enough against them, but for those who do enjoy them there is more defiant celebration of them as the solution to Christmas, the fulfillment of fantasy than evaluation of them as they connect or disconnect to/from domesticity, friendship, love.

When I hear gay men say, as I often have, "My friends are more important to me than my lovers," I am not sure what I am hearing. Either betrayal is so inevitable and painful in sexual relationships that it is best to make as little emotional investment as possible, or sex itself has so little importance as an expression of the whole person, it is rather more like eating and excreting than like talking and working. In either case, sex is seen as something apart from significant relationship, probably inimical to it because, if taken seriously, it can inspire deadly possessiveness and jealousy, kill spontaneity and therefore desire itself. The very sexual practices indulged in, introduced into an important relationship could reduce it to play-acting on other levels, infantilize it. The best that can be achieved in sexual exchange is mutual self interest, not the genuine altruism of what we call love. That is reserved for friendship.

It's a saner solution than many for disposing of sexual energy. It certainly compares favorably to the more accepted practice of encouraging young men to go off and get killed in foreign wars. But it is not a life-long answer. Youth and good looks are coin of a kind. A taste for boys who ask to be paid may be a way of prolonging that stay in sexual infancy, or it may be a way of moving to a more complex relationship that has to admit affection, protection, material responsibility. Most adults learn their first altrusim in the love of children, whether there is sexual involvement or not. Women freely admit erotic responses to their nursing infants, though the shock of their love is not that delicious intimacy but the sacrifice of time, sleep, sometimes nearly of sanity itself to serve that infant dependence. Children, however, grow up and leave home. If they are not our own, they're unlikely to return home with children of their own to share with us.

Gay men who restrict themselves to recreational sex fear the loneliness of aging, work hard to keep themselves fit and attractive to postpone the time when they buy their pleasure or go without.

Divorcing sex from love has real but temporary virtues. If we had been allowed to explore all those avenues of desire as children, the exercise might not have any attractions for us, but certainly most of us aren't ready to take our sexual selves into altruistic love when we're in our twenties. The question is what sort of sexual experience not only delights us when we're young but prepares us for a satisfying life when we're older. Is it a fantasy to want to arrive at fifty or sixty or seventy whole rather than drained, rich in experience rather than made cynical by it?

Women, for all the greater sexual restraints placed on us, are not so deprived in infancy and childhood of physical affection. Our vanity is encouraged, our interest in our own bodies validated by others' interest. And we aren't as long trapped in childish bodies as boys are, who must work for their muscles while we simply watch our breasts grow.

Though some lesbians envy gay men their sexual freedom, their parks and baths, most of us are uncertain that we have the same kind of sexual childhood to discover and live through. Conditioned from the beginning to think of our bodies as instruments to give pleasure and life to other people, our first rebellion is against the male eroticism imposed on us, that sexual urgency so often indifferent to us as people or our threatened futures. Recreational sex between women can seem simply a reenacting of male indifference that has been so threatening to us. For we haven't been deprived of sexual experience so much as bullied by it. All any female has to do is to indicate that she is available, for, as so many men have pointed out, we're all the same in the dark.

What many women want most of other women is mothering, that protective, attentive anticipation of all needs in order to serve them. In the safety of that care and love, eroticism flowers. Infant narcissism is at the center of our awakening sexuality. The older woman, therefore, is attractive. The complaint of younger women in bars is that so few older women go to them. The complaint of older women about the bars is that they are filled with children. Female teachers are so often erotic objects for female students because they are mother substitutes. Women who are mothers are attractive to other women for that reason. The cry of nearly every woman, whether to her husband, her children or her female lover is, "Grow up!" In her presence no one wants to; yet her own needs are often as infantile as theirs, for a change to be cherished, served, protected unconditionally.

Women, therefore, aren't so much inclined to separate sexuality from significant relationships as to isolate sexuality in love, to possess and be possessed so thoroughly that they are finally forced to leave home for the sake of their adult selves. *Sita* is a classic study of that process. For just as the infant fantasies of the baths don't translate easily into adult friendship, so infant dependency also inhibits adult love.

There are those of us who want to live alone. "I enjoy my own company," my eighty-eight-year-old neighbor says, who has always lived alone. The work of growing and changing sexuality is not always worth it for poeple with other commitments and goals which seem to them finally more important. But for others of us, discovering that sex can become something other than a sport or a dependency is important because we have learned that by means of it we can express tenderness, compassion, joy, wonder, and serenity, even though we are, therefore, more vulnerable to frustration, pain and grief. Because we are sexual creatures, we are mortal. Our bodies are not simple playthings. Our bodies die. To learn to live in them fully while we have the opportunity involves risk and care.

Hatred of the body and fear of death have inspired most of our culture's morality. Love of the body and love of life seem to me good alternatives for beginning again.

On a Moral Education

From the time we confront a sexuality that is labeled sick and sinful by conventional morality, we face a conflict which has driven some of us to suicide, some to psychiatrists, some to uncomfortable closets, and some to open rebellion. Accused of being immoral or at least amoral, very few of us, I think, accept that label. Sexual crusaders, like all crusaders, have an important moral investment in their cause. It is our morality rather than our lack of it that is frightening, understandably so, for the morally passionate have done more than their fair share of damage in the past. To be morally committed is not necessarily to be good; as Yeats points out in "The Second Coming":

> The best lack all conviction, while the worst
> Are full of passionate intensity

To persuade ourselves and then other people that we aren't "the worst," infecting society with our own disease, bringing about a decadence through which our culture, if not the world, will end, we have a great deal of work to do.

Our beginnings as rebels are personal. We accept the evidence of our senses and emotions against the negative platitudes of our upbringing and nearly immediately discover what a confusing, lonely and finally terrifying position that is, for, if we reject the conventions of sexual morality, what hold has any morality on us? Why not cheat, steal, rape, and murder? Once any part of a code of behavior is rejected, the whole structure is threatened and can collapse. There are people who live and die in the rubble of those broken commandments. Others take on the task of building again, determined to invent a structure in terms of which life makes better sense. If I may quote Yeats again, frankly out of his context:

> All things fall and are built again.
> And those who build them again are gay.

Questioning conventional morality can be the beginning of a moral education from which we can learn to make choices based on understanding rather than blind faith or great fear. The study of history makes it clear that the moral manipulation of people has rarely been for their own individual good but for the convenience of those institutions of power, church and state, who never have liked a questioning habit of mind not easily intimidated. We are dangerous not in what we do—though our acts will be decried and punished—but in that we feel free to choose at all.

Some of us, not understanding that it is our autonomy rather than a given behavior which is threatening, try to explain ourselves in terms designed to appease. "Look, we're really just like you. We have jobs. We pay taxes. Some of us have kids. And most of us are home in bed by ten o'clock, even on weekends. It's only the behavior of the outlandish radical fringe that keeps us from being accepted." Others of us recognize that, until the whole perception of sexuality is challenged and changed, we will go on being discriminated against, silenced, and jailed.

Our knowledge of our own bodies has been grossly distorted by lack of information, misinformation, superstition, and terror. From birth, though our sex is the most important social fact about us ("Is it a boy or a girl?"), we are trained away from bodily pleasures by parents scandalized at a six month old girl's learning to masturbate, at a nine month old boy's making a wall painting of his excrement. In fact, all our bodily education is a repeated insistence that we unlearn any pleasure we might discover until we are legal adults, at which time, under very limited circumstances, we may express our sexual ignorance to each other in all the disastrous clumsiness that we are beginning to confess, amused, rueful, outraged, depending on the nearly blind luck of our long delayed initiations. Of course, most of us don't wait as long as that. The marriage bed is not the simple horror it was a couple of generations ago. Still what we ask of our young is to be sexual adults when they have not been allowed to be sexual children. It's rather like expecting them to have successful college careers when we have continually forbidden them to learn to read.

We are so ignorant of sexuality that even those of us who would advocate positive sexual education of children aren't all that sure what exactly we'd teach them. Our job, first, is to educate ourselves. And we do have to begin by admitting how little we know, how much of that little is colored by fear and moral confusion.

Perhaps the greatest difficulty in a paper like *The Body Politic* for carrying on a discussion rather than a series of diatribes is that men and women, by nature and/or nurture seem to have very different sexual needs, and, since its readers are homosexual, there doesn't seem such an urgent need for understanding those differences. But politically it seems to me very important for us that we do. If we do, we may avoid spurious moral debate over what is really a difference in tastes, developed by different kinds of experience out of different natures.

The central moral issue about any sexual practice that

involves more than one person is consent. Consent is not an easy concept, for consent is given for a large variety of reasons, from simple desire to participate in pleasure to the far more complex motivations like a need to please, a fear of refusing, a wish to be humiliated and hurt, a desire to be politically correct, and so on. Very often, in ignorance, we aren't aware of our real motivations, much less the motivations of other people. Even if we are, we don't have moral education enough always to choose wisely either involvement or retreat. That there is no set of rules to apply doesn't mean we are not in a moral circumstance. Every kind of encounter with another person is a moral circumstance.

Sex involving people who otherwise don't know each other is, between men apparently, often a simplifying of the moral circumstance, isolating pleasure from as many other motivations as possible, from as many other meanings as possible, a celebration of the body's needs and desires without any other intention at all. That a lot of psychic need, guilt and other personal baggage may be carried into such encounters is something that can be acknowledged or not. It is not part of the contract.

I have heard a few women wish that we had parks and baths, places as frankly sexual as those available to men. Is it only our lack of money, of aggressive initiative, of courage that prevents us from creating such an environment for ourselves? I think it's more complicated than that. We don't really know how much is biological, how much is cultural, but most women seem to need to complicate sexual encounter with motives beyond pleasure for the pleasure to be available to us at all. Impersonal sex for us is rape, not liberation. How much we carry, even as lesbians, of a sense of our bodies as houses of birth, pledges to a future, may always inhibit us from the simple celebration of the sexual present. Or anyway, we have to work harder at it, rationalize against our knowledge and need of consequences to make love for pleasure alone, with anyone. Our desire is not so easily roused by physical beauty, prowess, sexual potency, as it is by need, vulnerability, tenderness.

Scatological humor along with a passion for cleanliness have been for years bewilderments about male behavior for me. "Bathroom jokes" my mother used to call them, indulgent of a male need to mock his bowels as a way to assert them. Most women don't have the fascination that men do for excrement. I'm suspicious of the explanation that shit is all men can create out of their bodies while women can graduate to babies. I ponder with reluctance as well the notion that men need to rebel all their lives against toilet training, for we were trained, too. Our other secretions are less regulatable. Our tabooed blood cannot be dismissed in a few minutes a day. We either must be isolated or carry that draining around with us, but it is the blood of possible life, and we know it. Blood is an image of injury or death for men.

Even in such radical statements as those about the pleasures of male fist fucking, there is fastidious preparation to clean the anal canal. In radical female sexuality, there is no such concern, rather a celebration of odors and secretions as erotically potent, women as source of the fluids of life.

Again Yeats made the point in his "Crazy Jane Talks With the Bishop":

> But Love has pitched his mansion in
> The place of excrement.

Women, speaking to men, are judgmental mothers saying, "Will you please keep your shit in the toilet?" or wives saying "Will you please stop your infantile requests that we light your farts?" or mothers of their children saying, "Surely you don't have to be so squeamish that you can't change a diaper."

Straight men often like the idea of making women pregnant, scoring points of potency, and the condom's wide acceptance is not as a device for birth control so much as a male protection against the "uncleanness" of a woman's body. Much of lesbian literature which deals with women leaving marriage for relationships with other women celebrates a new acceptance of the female body and female sexuality, free of pornographic pictures and other mechanistic approaches to sex, free of deodorizers, free of standards of performance.

Women are so generally put off sado-masochistic practices that predominantly male publications like *The Body Politic* and *The Advocate* are left to publish women who are interested in it. Because sado-masochism has been the undisputed norm of marriage until very recently with women the victims without reference to their own tastes, it has become politically so incorrect an idea as to be taboo. The argument that it is basically fantasy consented to and therefore harmless does not persuade. For economically dependent women, consent is a nearly meaningless word. Our revolutionary desires are for relationships free of power-tripping, free of notions of ownership and dependence.

In contemplating sexual relationships between children and adults, women are generally much more conservative than men for several reasons. Many women were sexually abused as children, usually by men. They are also chiefly responsible for the protection of children. Often feeling sexually exploited by men themselves, they are mistrustful of men's ability to be sexual educators of children, though recreational sex which men enjoy might, in fact, be a real pleasure for children, if the burdens of guilt and fear and ignorance were removed.

These are just a few of the areas in which men and women tend to disagree. If we are to work together toward a new understanding and acceptance of sexuality, we must avoid as much as possible black and white arguments about our differences in taste, becoming increasingly defensive and stupid.

Women can be more narrowly political about sexuality than will serve their understanding and freedom. Men can value rebellion for its own sake, justifying damaged lives in the name of courage to experiment. We must not be so beleaguered as a sexual minority that we defend our mistakes, for we are all sexual blunderers, only crudely understanding what sexuality is and how it can be used in the larger context of our lives. We must have critical courage if we are to arrive at sexual expression which is what Auden called writing poems, "sacred play."

Rule Making

I once taught at a boarding school where at the end of each year all rules, except those to do with physical safety, were crossed out so that in the fall students returned free to use their own judgment until such time as it seemed necessary to make a rule because too many students were staying up and out too late, because there were too many injured animals left in the biology lab, because too many of the day students' dogs were attending classes.

We are as much rule- as tool-making creatures because few of our behavior patterns are handed to us in our genes, and we need not only to shape our environment but get along with each other to survive. I suppose, because I moved around the continent a lot when I was a child, I learned early that, though all communities have rules, they are not the same ones in, say, suburban California and rural Kentucky. So I grew up with some respect for the necessity of rules but also with some critical distance from any particular rule's usefulness or moral justification.

I was delighted to find that, though a few rules at the boarding school cropped up early and regularly, a fair number did not recur. Since my father as a student made a practice of breaking rules not yet written, I always had special admiration for those students with the creative imagination to set the rule-makers to work on such things as not turning off the water mains into the teachers' quarters or taking the school tractor to church. I was also amused at the Head Mistress's rule every year that no student be allowed to get up at 4:30 a.m. on Patriots' Day to witness the reinactment of Paul Revere's ride. It was the only way she could be sure that students would think it worthwhile to lose sleep for an historic event.

Though some people and some communities thrive on absolutes, most of us under rigid regulation chafe and pine, and the chafers are more apt to resort to destructive than creative rebellion, the piners to waste away. Unless there is some compelling and overriding reason, therefore, people's behavior should be codified as little as possible.

As lesbians who have until very recently had no community, whose relationships have been themselves considered immoral if not criminal, we are for the first time in a position of declared responsibility, able to join together, able to describe for ourselves what the nature and value of our relationships are. We should not be surprised at how raggedly we have begun that process.

Many of us have internalized the larger community's prejudice and take any failure as an indication that we are, after all, sick and depraved. I have had letters from ex-lesbian nuns begging me to repent. Many of us feel very much on the defensive and want to justify our relationships by mimicking monogamous marriage and making strong statements against such things as promiscuity and seduction of the young. I've been having some correspondence with ex-nun lesbians who want to label the seduction of a nun by a sixteen-year-old student child abuse. Those with a more secular grounding often muddle through, as most other people do, in serial monogamy until over the years at any large party most women, at one time or another, have been lovers with most other women and call their community, either affectionately or sourly "incestuous." There are also those who think coupling is reactionary, the image of bondage that women, and particularly lesbians, should reject, who live alone or in groups, taking their pleasure where they find it. Recently one of the most vocal groups celebrates bondage as the most intense sexual fantasy to be fulfilled, the real declaration of freedom from puritanical hypocrisy. With them we come full circle, for they share with those in religious orders the strictest and most specific rules in search of ecstatic experience.

It must be clear to any lesbian who has been around a while that consensus is impossible. Our sexual preference gives us no more in moral common than it does our heterosexual sisters. Our chief reason for wanting to reach consensus is to defend ourselves against judgments from both without and within our community. The ex-nuns trying to make their sister ex-nun confess to child abuse say to her, "Isn't it better to be confronted by loving lesbians than by Christian homophobes?" to which her answer is, of course, "No, it's much, much worse."

Rules made to defend ourselves against those who disapprove of us are suicide weapons, for they serve to distort and then silence what we learn from our own experience, whether we are embracing those rules for ourselves or imposing them on other people. And they are also useless for our defense, for nobody who thinks a lesbian is sick and depraved will be persuaded of our health and virtue even if we set age limits, time limits, and correct postures.

As in that boarding school, I wish we could begin without rules, except those to do with physical safety, make rules only when they seem necessary and start afresh every year or so.

When I refer to "our community," it is a metaphor. We don't live under one roof, in one city, or even in one country. We, as lesbians, don't have to get along as we do with people who share a geography, property, and all the mundane chores of citizenship. The only rule I'd like to propose for "our community" is tolerance because we certainly have been getting into bad squabbles on the public platform and on paper. Oh, we can disagree all we like, but none of us needs to convert the whole world to separatism, monogamy, sado-masochism, or celibacy for the freedom to choose for ourselves, and each of us has more to learn about other choices without feeling personally threatened by them.

The problem is much more complex when we confront differences between people attempting to be friends and lovers.

One rule which is gaining support, particularly among younger lesbians, is the eliminating of power in relationships between women in an attempt to get away from the inequality of heterosexual models. Not only must concepts of butch and femme be banished, but women should seek out other women as much like themselves as they can. Look-alike, feel-alike, and think-alike couples are becoming so common that they may be the forerunners of the arranged marriages of the past with the same drawbacks because they infect any community with the snobberies of race, class, education, money, health and good looks. Further, power is not in this way eliminated, for power trips are not sourced in differences but in the simple desire of a person to dominate or be dominated.

It is not power but its abuse which should concern people. If one member of a couple is much stronger than the other, it doesn't necessarily follow that the weaker one will be physically abused. It may mean instead that nobody has to be hired to move heavy objects around. If one member of a couple is much brighter about figures, it doesn't necessarily follow that one will control the money. She may simply be stuck with doing the income tax returns. For strength and gifts are there to be of service in any loving circumstance.

The line in the marriage service, "for better or worse, for richer or poorer," which has trapped far too many people in destructive relationships does have the virtue of reminding us that both circumstances and people change. Even if two people start out in a relatively equal relationship, one may eventually make much more money than the other, be faced with a disabling disease, become famous, have to assume responsibility for an aging relative. Any of those changes would certainly break up a relationship based on a canceling balance of power.

People in love do have enormous power over each other, and it is often unequal simply in the quality of caring. Sylvia Townsend Warner wrote of her lifelong lover, Valentine Ackland, ". . . yonder sits the other one, who had all the cards in her hand—except one. That I was the better at loving and being loved." It was a relationship that survived sexual infidelity, separation, financial hardship, impossible mothers, war, Valentine's conversion to Catholicism, not without periods of strife and pain but with a great deal of productive work (both women were writers) and happiness. Sylvia Townsend Warner knew how to use rather than abuse her power to love and be loved.

People who want to be sure that they are always free to be and do as they please might be better off living alone, and increasing numbers do, in love with their work or their leisure, setting up a network of friends dependable in emergencies like illness or Christmas.

Only people unafraid of power, willing to risk being vulnerable to it and to take responsibility for it are real candidates for serious relationship, and some of the most unlikely ones from the point of view of those who look for equality are the most successful. To acknowledge difference, otherness, is the beginning of real love in which each can be depending and dependable according to her own gifts and needs.

If a relationship lasts richly, the rules do have to change whether they have to do with who takes out the garbage, who pays the rent, what goes on or doesn't go on in bed. I watch the earnest sweetness of one old woman learning to cook for the first time because her mate is recovering from an operation. (I wrote "lover," crossed it out, and wrote "mate" because I don't know whether they do make love or ever have, but I do know they have lived together and loved each other for probably forty years.) I watch myself learning sight-reading against long failures at that skill because Helen Sonthoff, the woman with whom I have lived for nearly thirty years, is having increasing trouble with her eyes. Now that she's retired, she's learned to tend the household machines so long my domain in order to give me more time to write. But it is not simply old age which changes patterns, makes new demands. Every period of living presents changes and problems no one could foresee, just as each lively one of us breaks rules which have not yet been written. I have now been forbidden to buy raffle tickets and put Helen's name on them. I have done it out of embarrassment at junk and craft sales when I find nothing else to buy, but the result has been prizes of unspeakable taste and uselessness. Cooking, reading, and raffle tickets may seem frivolous examples, but love is based in daily living which can be made up of petty disagreements and silly power trips or co-operation and laughter. In any couple both people can be comically overqualified for a job at hand or jointly defeated by changing a washer. Initial differences may minimize those puzzles. Willingness to change, to learn something new overcomes most of them.

The defeating issues, fidelity, politics, money, responsibility for others, may call up our rule-making instincts, and they may be necessary from time to time for a time. I read the other day that Frida Kahlo agreed to remarry Diego Rivera, accepting his infidelities, as long as he gave up his conjugal rights and paid no more than his share of the housekeeping, an odd bargain many of us would think, but it redefined their relationship enough for them to stay together to nourish each other in their work as no one else could.

Fairmindedness is not a simple talent, for each person's needs and desires are not only different but changing. There is no point in a second car when only one person knows how to drive. There is no point in the same number of lovers if only one wants them. Equal time in an argument is useless for a person who doesn't like to argue and is no good at it. Balance is probably more a matter of keeping one's own to help insure the balance of the other in the sometimes rocking boat.

I am very leery of any rule that is made after asking, "What would happen if . . . ?" I am on surer ground with "This has happened. Now what?" It is both realistic and affectionate to know that most rules really are made to be broken. A father left his son a series of notes about a box of cookies I had baked for them. The first said, "Jimmy, don't touch this box." Then inside the box, another note said, "Jimmy, don't eat these cookies." Finally on the bottom of the box, a note said, "Jimmy, leave me at least four cookies." When I next saw the box, four cookies remained. Fair enough.

PART III:

PROFILES AND RECOLLECTIONS

This Gathering

In my newly made study, two of the five paintings are by
Judith Lodge. The smaller one, "Dream with House, Bed and
Scraper," is also on the cover of my collection of short
stories. I don't know the name of the larger painting. Sometimes, as I lie on the couch, looking at it, I recognize it as
a source for what I will go on writing: the figure of a woman,
dressed in her own flesh, intent before a camera, has posed
globes of various sizes and colors, worlds to choose among
or take together. The enclosing surfaces of that space support continents threatened by the grid of latitudes which
do not measure so much as limit shapes otherwise fluid as
the amoeba, fetuses in the water belly of the world. When
John Reeves came to take my picture for *The Canadian*,
he floated my head and shoulders like an uncertain balloon
before the deep, flat blue as fiercely painted as a cement
floor, so that the figure of the woman with the camera can
still be seen. I should ordinarily be disturbed to find myself interrupting a painting, but, when I saw a proof of
that photograph, I remembered the opening of Judy's first

Vancouver show, and I found the paragraphs I had written shortly after it.

"The surface of the canvas is disturbed. Sometimes by a refrigerator door opening into visceral but nearly colorless interiors. Sometimes being torn and folded into or patched upon itself. Or the edge is defied, a line leaping to the new space of an adjacent canvas, leaving the tightrope walker on a wriggling, escaping journey. The surface of the figures is disturbed, bone jutting out of cheek or jaw, transparent skin revealing the sack or organs, of blood, of straining muscle. The animals invade, transform each other, camel becoming swan, swan emerging out of the head of a man. The mat of a drawing is cut to accommodate the tail feathers of a bird in a parade of creatures, walking, leading, following, into space beyond. Even the great, serene, flat colors could, it is understood, suddenly open by means of doors or tearings or cuttings and expose not the white gallery wall but the interior force and fear of distance or intimate mortality. Or a leaf, sticker or balloon could come forward insisting. The strong threatened surface across which objects and creatures pass, out of which they emerge, into which they disappear, is, even when it looks like a wall, much more like sky or sea or skin, the breaking container of life.

"We are all at home in this space because we are its raw materials as well as its inhabitants. We behave in terms of its hard and wonderful laws. John's head emerges from a drawing, joins his body and walks about the room. Larry stands like a mirror reflecting his own image. The sleeping woman, her blood gathering, is also an image in Shelagh Day's paper on sexuality, one of the ways she can talk about what it is to be a woman. We are a community of friends, together experiencing our communal biography, remembering, interpreting, sharing experience and work, time and space, as we do food and love."

Lives can close down, become contained in private houses, I in my study, Judy in her new white studio, but even in our solitudes we are aware that the walls may open into journeys, familiar faces, wounds, birth. The closing down and opening are the breathing rhythm of community, the washing blink of sight. There is no one of us so private at any time that we do not also walk with Judy's tightrope walker, camel walker, birds on parade, or peer out of her canvasses at our friends' serious regard, at ourselves.

My head can float in the John Reeves photograph, part of the on-going collage of our lives which I first saw that night. Our crafts are solitary, and yet we participate in each other's making. A new book waits inside a canvas to be born; words adhere to a globe. Here we gather again.

Judith Lodge, a Profile

A pale pink van, which Judy calls "the kleenex box," wheels into the yard of our Galiano house, and Judy opens the unusually wide back doors to get out her projector and slides, as well as six bottles of scotch I asked her to bring to our liquor-storeless island. She has come for two days to talk about her work. Inside the van are not only those expected items but four enormous canvases. "This is the new work you haven't seen," Judy explains as she drags out the first 4' x 8' canvas and carries it into the house. When she has unloaded them all, the living room is an entirely different place, the four canvases forming two 8' x 8' walls, "The First Gate" and "The Water Wall." This is the beginning of a new series called "The Walls of Eden," which will finally be a dozen paintings this size, to be shown at the Pender Street Gallery in September, 1977. It is the first major project in her new studio, added last summer to her house in Vancouver. She will be working on it six days a week, sometimes as long as eight hours a day, until it is done. She doesn't rest on the seventh day. She goes to the University of Victoria every Tuesday, getting up at five o'clock in the morning in order to meet the first of the two art classes she'll teach that day, returning late at night to Vancouver. It provides not only an extra source of income (she has a Canada Council grant this year) but a lively contact with students which she enjoys. The willful energy necessary to maintain such a weekly schedule explains why Judy doesn't hesitate to bring two 8' x 8' walls with her on a visit.

Before she has finished wedging newspapers under corners, bracing one pair against the fireplace, Judy has begun to talk about the dream fragment written in her notebook in 1972 which is the source of this whole series. It begins in a cafe at night. The friend with her is sick and feverish; a truck is dumping snow into the basement of the building. A door opens onto a room whose walls are painted in hot fluorescent colors, which move out into the room. A beautiful, hot pink snake makes Judy realize that these are the walls of Eden.

As she tells the dream, I look at "The First Gate," flickering in fire colors which warm the room as well as the fire we won't now be able to have, tropical green deeper in, blooming with the colors of parrots. Two large, hard-edged Xs bar the way, and a grid like a rising gate occupies the upper fifth of the canvas.

I have been looking at Judith Lodge paintings for some years, and she anticipates my surprise at the absence of the human figure, the subject which characteristically preoccupies her. "The painting was getting too heavy, too heavy-handed. There was so much emotional, autobiographical information in those figures, I got so I couldn't tell what was wrong when it was wrong; whether an image was emotionally confused or technically diffused." So she has made a decision to banish figures from her paintings for at least six months in order to concentrate more wholly on aesthetic and technical problems. When the figures are allowed back in for the later paintings in this series, Judy expects to greet them with a larger vocabulary and a new environment. There will not be the strong contrast between the large, flat areas and the embellished figures which created the compelling tension of much of Judy's earlier work but also finally has become too limited, technically and emotionally, for what she wants to do now. "There has been a kind of ambiguousness, translucence, in the images I've used so far that evokes a scary response. When people said 'horror' and I hadn't thought 'horror,' I still couldn't say, 'I didn't intend that,' because a lot of what I've done does strike the same emotional note."

As we look at the slides Judy has brought over, I see again many of the paintings I've see in her Vancouver shows at the Bau Xi Gallery in 1973, 1974, and 1975, and there are paintings and drawings from earlier shows at Skidmore College in 1971, where she taught from 1969 to 1972, and at Wheelock College in 1972. There are a lot of isolated figures, figures isolated from each other. There is grandeur as well as pain in many of the male figures, who are often regally robed. I think of them as wounded kings, rigidly flat, remote. The female figures are innocent of that grandeur, made of translucent flesh through which there are suggestions of organs, blood, vulnerable, often accompanied by fecund images of eggs, globes. I ask Judy if she looks differently at these paintings now after so much exposure to the women's movement.

"Yes, of course. Some of them scare me now. I am always so literal. That's part of putting away the figure for a while."

Many of the paintings are not in that hard place, however, though they represent the strongest of her work to date. There are the elegant hands and hand puppets, the masks which are more playful and joyful than frightening, and more recently the whole series of paintings of the woman artist, represented with a camera, photographing the Banff mountains, where Judy has been a visiting artist in the summer for several years, photographing family groups. Not among the slides because the original hangs in my study is the painting of the woman artist in her studio, photographing an arrangement of world globes, the studio walls rich with the shapes of continents. The figure here is also translucent flesh, but the stance is intent, almost aggressive, the line of the focusing arm graceful and active as a gesture in dance, reminiscent of the swan necks in earlier paintings. Dressed in its own flesh, the figure seems not vulnerable so much as erotic. The images of the studio are still more substantial than the figure intent upon them, their surfaces richly embellished with collages, depths of paint in rich colors. It is, as many of Judy's paintings are, an object to be touched as well as looked at. When she sees it again, her hand greets it nearly as quickly as her eye. She wants to touch the brush work of the hair because there the paint is thinner, the brush strokes light and free. "That's one of the textures I want now," she says.

"It hasn't all been one tone," I say.

"No, but I mistrust some of the elegance in the earlier ones. The ones I care about can get overworked sometimes, but these others . . . it's so easy to be seduced by what's beautiful."

I look again at the new walls. "The Water Wall" is blue, alive with thin spray gestures, with fans of vibrating lines, the grid in this one so high and light in the painting it might almost be floating away. There is gold, "precious and religious" for Judy with the attendant danger of the beautiful. The painting *is* beautiful.

"Well," Judy laughs, "the grid is going to go finally." We've been watching it as it began in horizontal lines in a 1970 drawing and became fences, window frames, the longitude and latitude of maps, a grid sometimes imprisoning most of a painting. "I'll be glad," she says, "finally to get rid of it, but I do like the clear tension of those lines. I do like what they can do."

The psychological and technical are not separated in the paintings or in Judy's talk about them. The tension between polarities, whether between sharp hard lines and vulnerable surfaces, between inside and outside, between images of fire and water, is where she locates the energy of painting. "Like being in the center between two magnets," because what threatens to pull apart also holds a painting together.

The whole of one of Judy's Vancouver shows was devoted to paintings sourced in dreams, and, since a dream fragment is also the basis for a new series, I ask her why she so often uses that subject matter, not expecting, because I have talked with Judy often, a treatise on Jung. I am not disappointed at the simple answer. "It's so much the space my head is in anyway in the studio." Sleep, for Judy, is obviously kin to the solitude of work, dream images its natural vocabulary.

Judy has spread a number of black and white drawings on the floor, which she completed last summer in Maine to be reproduced in the January issue of *The Canadian Fiction Magazine*. Though the figure is still present, the absence of color forces attention on texture. "The chief problem with black and white is that the drawing gets darker and darker." Again her hand moves to those areas of the drawings where the ink is sparing, quick, full of energy. Once color is introduced into such a texture, the control has to be exact, particularly in reds, oranges, and pinks, or a painting can catch fire. "It's like painting with sparklers." There are two entries in Judy's notebook, poems, matched polarities of red and green. The first recalls children setting fire to a field, only with the intention of keeping warm, the inadvertant and frightening result. The second is a view of that field as the new green shoots begin, the contours of the land still visible, like the skull of a child who has had a crew cut. We look back for a moment into Judy's childhood in St. Paul, Minnesota, the small wilderness near her house which she first began to sketch without wondering whether she could do it, was any good at it, simply needing to show how she felt about it. There on the floor before us are strong, delicate, dark trees, around us the first walls of Eden. "These images," Judy says of some in the ink drawings, "could be much, much larger and still work."

"Is large scale a test?" I ask.

"It's about knowing where the boundaries are," Judy says. "It's important now that the scale could be large."

On such vast surfaces as these walls, Judy uses large brushes, sponges, edges of rulers. She sometimes has to stand on a chair to reach. Because of the nature of the acrylics she uses, she must work quickly and for long hours. The boundaries are not simply the limits of the canvas but Judy's own physical limits. It occurs to me that she is not painting pictures of the dream but recreating it so that she can literally walk into it. "Eden is a kind of clear and whole place to be, being closer to light, fire, water, green, growing, different from being in a room."

"It's a moral vision," I say.

"Yes, oh yes," Judy agrees. She talks about what she calls her biases and prejudices, how frightening it is to her to see an intellectualized aesthetic and great skill employed without reference to subject matter, without a real vision. When Judy was a student at MacAlester College in St. Paul, content was nearly irrelevant, the gods deKoonig, Klein, Stella. In her four years there, a life class was never offered. She had to wait until she was working on her MFA at Cranbrook Academy of Art in Michigan for an opportunity to draw the human figure.

"How long does it take to recover from having been educated in an aesthetic hostile to your own?"

For Judy there was more involved than her need to use subject matter even when her instructors saw no point in it. Though her parents had provided their children with a good library and encouraged their interest in art, Judy was nearly alone in high school in her desire to do something more with her life than work at the dime store after school and marry as soon as possible after graduation. She found a good many of her courses difficult and beside the point. The Episcopal Church provided her with a sense of participation in ideas and images large enough to nourish her imagination. She loved the physical church, singing in the choir with her three younger sisters, the pageantry, and the discussions that took place at church conferences, but, by the time she went to college and began to study religion, the sermons she had tried to ignore (much as she now ignores the story line and even the sound of some movies which are visually marvelous) were too blatantly stupid and bigoted for her to tolerate. At the height of the Vietnam war, with black ghettos burning, suburban white middle class churches were more defensively insular than ever. Judy's leaving the church was a political act which did not separate her from what was precious and holy in the experience.

The climate of art classes was unsympathetic not only to the question of content but also to women, who could not be taken seriously as artists since they were expected to give up "all that" for marriage and raising children. Judy had to fight for financial help in graduate school. Then she watched the men in her class take all of the few jobs available in colleges. Patching a living out of occasional prizes and sales, she lived one year at home in order to paint, taught in a high school to get enough money for a year in Europe. When she finally did become an instructor of painting and drawing at Skidmore, her sense of accomplishment was soon threatened by the drain full-time teaching is on any artist, by the climate of negative competition; yet she wonders, if she had not finally been fired because the staff had to be cut back and she was a single woman who therefore didn't really need the job, whether she'd still be there. As with so many other strong and determined women, experiences which should be defeating become means to radical freedom.

For the last three years, since she was thirty-two, Judy has spent most of her time painting. Deprived of the material security and professional status of teaching, she discovered that there were ways of surviving from sales of paintings to the Art Bank, to the B. C. Provincial Art Collection, as well as to private collectors, from part time teaching, from grants. The driving will to vindicate herself has been transformed into working energy where a lot of the old questions about her right as a woman to be a painter fall away. A lot of the negative tension, a lot of the doubt, as she looks back, seems contrived, the result of having so little time to paint that the questions of what to paint and how to paint were false tests rather than real problems.

Judy spent enough time in the east to know she was uncomfortable there in the frenetic pace easterners believe in. Her decision to come to Canada was, first of all, for her own personal and psychic safety. Though she thinks of herself as political, wanting to know what is really going on, she does not know how responsible she can be with that knowledge. The decision of citizenship is still before her. For now, the only place she can feel entirely in control and responsible is alone in her studio. Her art is her statement in a threatened and threatening world.

The doors she is now working on as the entrance to "The Walls of Eden" are to be "formidable, difficult to approach, ornate, golden." but they are to be opened. The key is a line from Rilke in Judy's notebook: "I would like to walk out of my heart under the wide sky."

Takao Tanabe

Takao Tanabe was born in 1926 in Seal Cove, British Columbia, a small village about three miles from Prince Rupert, the fourth of six children born to Naojiro Izumi and his wife, Tomi Tanabe. Takao, like his brothers and sisters, was registered under his father's name. For the first fifteen years of his life he was Takao Izumi, son of a commercial fisherman. Seal Cove was the family's winter home. In the summer they moved to fishing camps on the Skeena River where the women and sometimes the children worked to prepare the catch. Though Tak can even now complain about the absence of beef from his family table, he retains his taste for the salmon, shrimp and crab he ate as a child. He fillets a fish with skill and pleasure, weaves a cedar basket for it and cooks it slowly out of doors over smoking alder branches as the Indians do. He can also pre-pare the Japanese dishes of his childhood. The parties he gives are feasts.

When Takao was eleven, the family moved to Vancouver. He lists as equal wonders flush toilets, streetcars, and library books, but he had less than five years to discover and enjoy the city. In 1941, after the outbreak of the war, all Canadians of Japanese descent were first required to register with the government. By a Japanese custom called 'yoshi' Tak's father, a third son, had agreed on his marriage to take his wife's name since she was an only child. Now he and his wife decided that the promise should be kept. At fifteen, Takao Izumi became Takao Tanabe and shortly after that his rights and privileges as a citizen, along with those of his family and all others of Japanese ancestry, were suspended. Herded into the P.N.E. grounds in Vancouver, families camped and waited for the B.C. Security Commission to assign them to what were euphemistically called 'relocation camps.' The older children in the family chose indentured farm work; so only Takao and his younger brother and sister went with his parents to Lemon Creek which was simply an empty farmer's field until the people built themselves small wooden shacks, heated by wood stoves. There were communal bath houses, and water was supplied by a pipe that ran along the road. They were allowed no radios or newspapers. There was no school for Takao to attend, and he lost interest in trying to complete high school by correspondence. He was occasionally employed to cut firewood or cedar shakes, but he was most of the time unemployed.

After two years in the camp, Takao was allowed to join an older brother and sister who, after a year as farm workers, had been permitted to move to Winnipeg. For two more years he was a labourer until he was accepted at the Winnipeg School of Art in 1946. Tak still regrets that Lemoine Fitzgerald, head of the school in 1946, did not teach first year students. Tak's only recollection of Fitzgerald is of a "tall balding silent man with gold rimmed glasses who occasionally smiled at us rather vaguely as he caught us sneaking out to play hookey." In 1947 Joseph Plaskett was appointed acting head to replace Fitzgerald. He had come from New York where he studied with Hans Hofmann. Joe was not only a major influence in Tak's decision to become an artist but also became his great friend. They took sketching trips together, and Joe, who shares with Tak a taste for the occasionally flamboyant and faintly ridiculous, would be a happy guest for a show opening Tak insisted on having one Halloween.

After graduating in 1949, Tak and some friends organized the Gimly Summer Art School, but there were only enough students registered for one large class, and after that summer Tak returned to earning his living as a laborer. Between 1950 and 1953, he worked at the Banff School of Fine Arts, the last summer promoted to foreman and laborer/handyman. Responsible for hanging paintings, he sometimes put up some of his own, and once he was given permission to take a course at the school. During the first winter he lived on unemployment cheques and went on painting. The Winnipeg School of Art had disbanded and the University of Manitoba had organized a Fine Arts department, staffed by a group of young American artists who arranged for Tak to have a studio space at the school.

The winter of 1951 Tak spent in New York studying with Hans Hofmann and Reuben Tam at the Brooklyn Museum Art School. In Tam he found another sympathetic teacher who gave him new insights into his work, but New York was second choice, a place that would always be there. What Tak had really wanted to do was go to Black Mountain College in North Carolina to study with Josef Albers. Since it was not on the Attorney General's approved list of schools, he could not get a visa. For a man of Tak's deep interest not only in art but in literature, that temporary and amazing place would have provided an exact atmosphere. The year in New York was, nevertheless, a success. Through John Cacere and Richard Bowman, new teachers in Winnipeg, Tak met Paul Brach and Mimi Schapiro, and with them Guston, Kline and others, all regulars at the old Cedar Bar on University Place.

Ten years after his forced departure from Vancouver, Tak returned to the city, uneasy with angers he was still trying to ignore, slurs against the Japanese in those days as common as anti-American comments are today, one of those "dirty, inscrutable Japs you couldn't trust" back trying to figure out how to live among people who had taken their lands, their boats, their livelihoods, as well as years of their lives. He worked with Robert R. Reid, the typographer, and became so proficient in graphic and typographic layout and design that over the years he could make a small living at it while leaving himself also free to paint. Eventually he bought himself an old press and founded Periwinkle Press which published, among others, John Newlove's early work, poems by Phyllis Webb and Roy Kiyooka, beautiful books which are now collector's items.

In 1953 Tak was awarded an Emily Carr Foundation scholarship, which allowed him to spend the next two years in Europe, based in London where he attended Central School of Arts and Crafts only long enough to satisfy the requirements of the scholarship, for his real purpose was to use those years in the galleries and museums of Europe to provide himself with a background in art history. On his very reluctant return to Canada in September of 1955, he met Patricia Anne White on board the S.S. Arosa Star. They were married in New York in March of 1956 and went to Winnipeg for six months before returning to Vancouver where Tak again worked with Robert Reid and painted while Patricia became a social worker.

A number of artists, writers and people associated with the arts founded the Arts Club of Vancouver in 1957. Tak was on the first board of directors and supervised the volunteer work crews who prepared the rented space for use. In those days, people like Lawren Harris and Jack Shadbolt could be found arguing over the choice of roller or brush for whitewashing a wall, and Geof Massey supplied the marble for the coffee tables. The Art Club has survived as a theatre club, but in its beginning it provided a place for people to share their work and their leisure, to make a community within a city notorious for its privacy and isolation. Abe Rogatnik's and Alvin Balkind's New Design Gallery shared the premises, and it was there that the Halloween opening took place, which Tak attended disguised as himself so that his friends would recognize him.

When Takao was awarded a Canada Council bursary in 1959, he and Patricia stored some of the few belongings they had accumulated and auctioned off the rest down to the last jar of pickles and the ironing board. They spent the next two years in Japan where Tak studied sumi-e with Ikuo Hirayama of the Tokyo University of Arts and calligraphy with Yanagida Taiun. Because Tak spoke fluent Japanese but had not learned to write it, in their extensive traveling through the country he was sometimes irritated to be mistaken for an illiterate native. And he was more impatient than Patricia when his relatives assumed her silence was due to his transforming her into a good Japanese wife rather than to her ignorance of the language. Patricia found it a peaceful interlude before she began to speak the language herself.

Another part of his lifelong education accomplished, with perhaps a clearer knowledge of his roots in the west, Tak came back again to Vancouver, and from 1961 to 1968 he and Patricia seemed to settle, building a house in West Vancouver, a cabin on a bit of shoreline up the coast. Tak joined the staff of the Vancouver Art School as head of the commercial art department, but he soon found teaching too absorbing and time-consuming, drawing as it does on the same energies he had reserved for his own work. One leave of absence, during which he intended to paint, was taken up entirely with work on a large commission for the Department of Agriculture, an enormous mural, housed in a warehouse on the north shore where friends would find him reeling under the strong smell of the glue he had to work with, bewildered that any school child would elect the experience. That project finished, he took yet another year's leave, but that, too, was partly devoted to a large commission for the Winnipeg Centennial Concert Hall. This time friends went to the great, gloomy Armories to watch the brilliant banners unfurled for *Weekend* photographers before they were shipped east.

A last year of teaching in 1967 convinced Tak that he had to leave not only that occupation but Vancouver, which had become too comfortable and too dull. Patricia was also restless with the limitations of her social work and planned to get her doctorate at Bryn Mawr. This time instead of an auction, there was a large feast, and the guests were required to take objects with them when they left, piles of doors on which Tak had painted or made collages of driftwood, an old bathtub he'd left in the front yard, claiming ambitions to enter the bathtub race. They were angry, comic emblems of rebellion against the middle-class security which had nevertheless engulfed them in their settled years in Vancouver, a pattern of living that had begun to separate Tak from his work.

Philadelphia, where Patricia settled to hard academic work, was not an environment for Tak. He moved to New York, found a loft in Soho which he transformed from a rough dirty shell into a working studio, and there he could devote himself to painting again though he had also to take jobs in carpentry and plumbing to supplement the small living he was making from his work. Invited to design Canadian stamps for commemorating Expo '69 in Japan, Tak failed to please the judges. He turned those designs into a series of metal buttons of the sort for campaigns and protests; like the doors they were emblems of anger that were beautiful.

It is no wonder that he understood so well the energetic anger and high good humor of the women's movement in those days in New York. Along with his own buttons, he wore theirs, and joined in the first great march.

The years between 1969 and 1972 were centrally important not only to Tak's direction as a painter but in establishing a clearer view for him of Canadian life and art.

Outside the country, he was still working on the hard edge geometric abstractions that had preoccupied him for some time, but he was gradually preparing himself for a change in both imagery and technique, which would coincide with his return to Canada.

Twenty years after Tak had been foreman and labourer/handyman at the Banff School of Fine Arts, he returned to teach at the summer school. In 1973, when Patricia received her Ph.D. from Bryn Mawr, Tak accepted the position of head of the art department at Banff. It is a job that suits him well. Administration, like plumbing and carpentry, takes planning and skill, but doesn't make the same demands that teaching does. He has at least six months free for his own work, and he is near the great prairie landscapes which provide the flat, simply divided areas, the basic imagery for his latest paintings, which achieve a seemingly effortless serenity. But he is also drawn to the east coast, where Patricia now teaches, and is looking for a barn there which might be converted into a studio. Or Ontario? Though the West Vancouver house has now been sold, there is still the cabin on that bit of British Columbia shoreline.

As a painter Tak has not become identified with the west coast, though he has spent a number of years here, nor will he become known as a prairie painter, nor as a painter of the eastern shoreline. Nor can he be identified as most painters of his established reputation are with any particular institution. The authority of his work is the claim he has laid on it to be the primary commitment of his life, wherever he is. He has also claimed Canada, a decision no institution or region could have brought him to. It is his own singular vision that has brought him home to the large landscapes across this large land that are his.

Preview

John Korner did not go to Nigeria last winter in search
of new images. He went to visit his younger daughter, Diane
Owen, and her husband, Stephen, both of whom were
sent by CUSO to teach for two years. Their school is located
near the tiny village of Waka; the nearest town of any size
is Biu, in Bornu State, northeastern Nigeria. Though Korner
has occasionally found subjects for paintings in the desert
or prairie and does sketches wherever he is, the prolific
body of his work, since his first Canadian show at the Vancouver Art Gallery in 1940, is a celebration of the landscape he lives in, the vivid flowers, great trees, the water,
mountains and sky of this northern coast. The serene energy
of his work most often comes in greens and blues and yel-
lows, glittering with natural light, explosive as seed pods
are, its rhythms those of wind and tide. Just before he left
on his long journey to an African Christmas, he said with
characteristic reluctance, "I never know why people go
anywhere else, once they are here."

The more than thirty paintings, oils, acrylics and water
colors, to be shown at the Bau Xi Gallery between September

5th and 17th have been as startling to the painter as they will be to those who know his work. Before when he has worked with hot, deep reds, the paintings have been oddly interior, a visceral introspection. The heat of these paintings is huge, one space expanding into another until there are tripychs of a landscape of such intense temperature that it literally bursts into flame. "They let the grass fires burn, except when they get too near the huts. I went out with Steve to help beat out the flames near their house and watched the birds hovering, waiting for small animals flushed out of their cover by the fires." The grasses, charred by fires, churned by winds, are as much force as fact. The figures of Nigerians move through the heat and rest in the shade of these landscapes. "It was like walking into Biblical times," life in the village a hard simplicity. Unused to such heat, with no way to escape it but in his own stillness, Korner spent his time absorbing the intensity of the experience for the paintings he has done since he has come back.

Though the radical contrast of climate and culture has jarred a number of Canadian artists into attempts to express an African experience, only those who can discover an affinity as well can capture something beyond tourist snapshots and vignettes. Korner, as an artist and a man, is a contemplative. Though he is very much at home here, he spent his boyhood in Czechoslovakia, and this raw, young world must have seemed in ways as strange to his European sensibility as Africa where he could at once recognize the long tradition of life, not broken and made invisible as it has been here. He is more native than stranger in the natural world. The human figure, when it appears, is always part of the much larger design of life, as are the roofs of houses, masts of ships, fragile hard edges against the rhythms of leaves and clouds. There is the same quality of mystic illumination in the African paintings that there is in his vision of this landscape, a letting of the natural fire be.

Diane and Stephen will be home in time to attend the opening of this show. Importantly it is a gift to them of an experience shared, but now that Korner has no domestic excuse to make the journey again, he watches these paintings and says quietly, "I want to go back to Africa."

John Korner

I have known three of John Korner's studios. The first, in the late fifties, on Adera Street in Vancouver, was like a doll house for royal children, set back toward the alley behind the vegetable garden. Most of the neighbors thought it was for John's two small daughters, Sidney and Diane. The second was on Kingston Avenue, out by the university where the family moved for the girls' college years. That was a converted two-car garage, attached to the house. Now John Korner paints in the fourth bedroom of an apartment ten floors up on Larch Street. Because place overwhelmingly dictates the images of Korner's paintings, much of his work can be dated by what he has seen in and from these three places, extended first by summers with the children at Crescent Beach or in the gulf islands, later by trips to Europe and Africa. Always he returns to the landscape he came to first in 1939.

John Korner was born in Czechoslovakia in 1913, to parents with professional expectations for their two sons. Even as a schoolboy, Korner was preoccupied with drawing and painting. He illustrated all his textbooks. While the school authorities reprimanded him for defacing books, his schoolmates asked him to illustrate theirs and often sold the results for chocolate bars. Though he took art classes, he was restless with the requirement to learn by copying. When he finished school, he was sent to Geneva to study law. After two years there, he persuaded his father to allow him to continue his law studies in Paris, where he could also quietly pursue his interest in painting. While there, he studied with Victor Tischler, Othon Friesz, and Paul Colin.

As for so many others of his generation, the threat of war obscured personal choices, and in 1939 Korner came to Vancouver to work in one of his family's lumber mills. He was in the personnel department at the mill when he married Eileen Newby in 1945. His young wife had no idea she had married an artist, for Korner had decided he must give up sketching and painting in order to concentrate on his new responsibilities. For six years he didn't paint at all, but, as is true of all real artists, he had not simply given up a skill and pleasure but his primary means of expressing a vision that informed his inner life.

While he was still in Geneva, a friend of his father's introduced him to the works of Bô Yin Râ, a painter and luminary whose spiritual teachings have been central to Korner's own development. Painting was the one means by which he could express the beauty of the natural world which is to him a reflection of a much greater spiritual reality.

In 1951, with his wife's blessing, Korner gave up his job in order to devote time to painting. In those early years, he also taught drawing and painting first at the Vancouver School of Art from 1953–58, then at the University of British Columbia from 1957–62. For the last twenty years Korner has had no distractions from his own work. He is represented in some thirty public collections in Canada and the United States, and he has had numerous one-man shows in Vancouver, Toronto, and Montreal as well as in the western United States. But such professional descriptions of his career don't adequately express either his real achievement or his goals which exist apart from worldly success.

Korner has written "a mere visual itinerary concerned only with material surroundings or even aesthetic considerations seems inadequate." He has sought a continuous awareness of that splendor in nature which can reveal the power of the spirit. Images in nature become metaphors, a testimony of the visions he experiences. John Korner's paintings, however, are not esoteric and can be easily identified as expressionist works. What distinguishes them is a sense of wonder that is exultant but not surprised in images as close as a flower, as distant as the stars, images available to all of us but illuminated for us by Korner's craft.

John Korner is not a man to speak often or at length about his work or his beliefs. I remember one of my first experiences with him which gave me some insight into his way of perceiving. We were walking back through his garden on Adera to look at some of his paintings, and he stopped by a small Japanese maple that had dropped all of its delicate scarlet leaves. "Like a pool of blood," he remarked quietly, and to this day I can see the skeletal branches of that tree, standing in the vivid fall of its own life. Nearly all of Korner's red canvases, even when they are apparently blooming flowers, express something of those hard transformations of birth/death/rebirth.

I bought my first painting of his on Adera, twenty years ago. It hangs above the desk where I work, an episode of light which is explosive not like a bomb but like a seedpod or breaking of a wave. What falls over a nearly obscured landscape is not destruction but benediction.

Another painting of his hangs in the living room, "the only cool spot in the room," he observes, against the warmth of cedar walls, rust carpet, brick fireplace, books and Indian baskets. The painting is called "Trincomali Channel," which lies between Galiano and Salt Spring Islands. It is a simplification of an already serene landscape of shore, sea and sky. The small white episodes on the beach could be shells or driftwood or the marking of a tidal chart, for it is both the actual place and an abstraction: the view as one studies the details of the shore and also looks off to the horizon, and also a chart or map of the place. I had to see the painting to recognize how I, and perhaps all of us, claim the land we know well with that trifocaled vision of it.

I have numerous drawings Korner has done not only here on Galiano but in New England and England on shared holidays. The east wall of an old farmhouse in New Hampshire, the back face of a suburban house we shared in Surrey, England, are faithful representations of a superbly confident draftsman documenting the places of our personal history. The Galiano sketches are more complex: a Boston rocker anchored to the corner of a room, framed in Indian baskets, becomes the inner spirit of an outdoor landscape of trees and sky shafted with light, again offering the multiplicity of vision any beloved place is, the many knowings becoming one aesthetic whole, the large intimacy of home.

When Korner moved to Kingston Avenue, his studio overlooked Burrard Inlet, punctuated by the lighthouse on the north shore which rises directly to mountains. He was still surrounded by the immediacy of flowers and worked long hours, as he had on Adera, in the garden, but always before him, when he looked up and out, was the entrance to the harbor. For years that convergence of land, sea, and sky, calm and light-struck or in wild weather, through the seasons, was his image of spirit welcome.

Now that he lives ten floors above ground, his horizon shifts to the distant mountains over the cityscape below, to the vast reaches of sky, the near surprise of flowers in buckets on the balcony.

Choosing images from foreign lands, Korner works more consciously at their evolving meanings. The tartans of Scotland become roofs of houses, patterns of fields, relieved by forces of living water, become lattice work, become the human pattern imposed, the order always giving way to moving light.

In Africa the human figure becomes a defining image, dark and brilliantly draped against the bleached land, which is fragile with heat, then ablaze with wind and fire, dark birds whirling away. They are not frightening paintings. They are alive with elemental energy, with what is both primordial and abiding in the human spirit. I wake every morning to a painting of African grass, aboil, a red sari streaming above in the drying wind like a banner against a sky bluegreen with heat. My own wash on the clothes line inherits significance.

Korner is one of the few painters I know who can introduce humor into a painting without turning it into a joke. While he was still on Adera, inside his garden views, he celebrated spring by incorporating seed packets of flowers and vegetables into his paintings so that, for instance, giant images of sunflowers bloomed out of a row of real sunflower seed packets glued to the bottom of the painting. I own my favorite of those lightly collaged paintings, the north shore mountains so suggestive of a nude woman in repose, outlined by a parade of very small black cats, cut from the newspaper movie advertisements where they warned that a film was restricted to adult viewing.

The spiritual intensity of Korner's work is often carried by seminal energy, the celebration of all that is alive, fertile, growing, transforming itself from seed to shoot, to leaf and flower, to exploding pod of new beginnings. The print of Bô Yin Râ's face of christ which has hung in all Korner's studios is not a prudish presence but a spirit both pure and all inclusive, incarnate flesh.

Poetry is an important source of nourishment for Korner. He turns often to the poems of Gerard Manley Hopkins. The 'inscape' of a Hopkins poem, which is both its spiritual source and its aesthetic rhythms, is recognizable also in Korner's paintings. I look at tartan fields and hear "landscape plotted and pieced- fold, fallow and plough," at one of the brilliant paintings of the coast glitter series and hear,

"It will flame out, like shining from shook foil." It is religous wonder Hopkins and Korner share: "He fathers forth whose beauty is past change:/ Praise Him." For both painter and poet, it is not so much the history or the myths of faith that are sources of inspiration as it is the living presence of the spirit in the world of nature.

Here on the west coast, all painters are landscape painters, whether they, like Emily Carr and John Korner, accept the great spiritual force of the convergence of forest, sea and sky or struggle against it periodically as Gordon Smith does, puzzling at how difficult it is to escape an horizon. In a frontier society, which British Columbia still essentially is, the heroes are the lumber barons, the road and bridge builders, the designers of skyscrapers, but we are fortunate that many of those people have come here, as Korner has, from older cultures which recognize the civilizing necessity of art, without which the spirit grows mean and then departs. We have begun to collect and share the great Indian artifacts which have informed this coast for centuries with mythic power, and Emily Carr who worked for so long without recognition is now one of our bridges to the totems and forests of their origin. She can even find celebration in a logged-off land where only several very tall and spindly trees remain among the stumps in "Scorned as Timber, Beloved of Sky." Here and there in a public building or a friend's living room we begin to discover paintings of the artists who live among us now, but our artists are not often allowed into the life of our city, our country. Like Emily Carr, they work in relative isolation, providing us with an inheritance which may not be generally recognized until our grandchildren or great-grandchildren require the visions that inhabit this place.

I have seen Korner walk on Galiano, showing his own grandchildren what his eyes have found, fungus, leaf on the forest floor, barnacle, clam and crab on the shore line. He has taught them also to look at paintings, beginning with the magic forests of Elizabeth Hopkins. They paint their own pictures for him, for as their grandfather has said, "There is an inborn need to create, and thereby to celebrate the world by metaphor and symbol."

To live among his paintings as I have done for so many years is to be in the presence of transforming light, visions that do celebrate a world as it is and as it may become if we can serve as perceiving creatures and know, "though the last lights off the black west went/ Oh, morning, at the brown brink eastward, springs—" John Korner is the painter of that dawning light.

Elisabeth Hopkins

In 1973 when the Bau Xi Gallery first invited Elisabeth Hopkins to show her watercolors, she was seventy-nine years old. At first she protested, "If I were young... if I were sixty..." Since that time she has had at least one show a year at the Bau Xi Galleries in Vancouver and in Toronto, and Talonbooks has published her children's story, *The Painted Cougar.* She has been photographed, interviewed, and written about more than interests her, but her mail lets her know that her example is an encouragement not only to the old but to the young daunted by the pressure to define themselves early. Though Elisabeth Hopkins has painted all her life, she did not have time to devote herself to it until she retired at seventy to Galiano Island from jobs as various as nursing and running a bookstore.

English by birth (she came to Canada when she was young, just before her sixtieth birthday), Elisabeth Hopkins is the step-granddaughter of Francis Ann Hopkins, well known painter of scenes of the Canadian wilderness, and cousin of Gerard Manley Hopkins, the English poet. She is interested not only in her famous relatives but in cousins she can turn up across the world, who arrive at her cottage door and at her openings, along with a growing number of devoted fans, among whom other artists and children are prominent. John Korner, who bought a small watercolor of hers at a Galiano group show, first introduced her to the Bau Xi Gallery, and she and Tony Onley have swapped watercolors. Drawings children have given her share wall space with misty Indian canoes by Francis Ann Hopkins, flowers by Molly Bobak, and the company often crowded into her small living room is that diverse, too.

Catholic but definite in her tastes, Elisabeth Hopkins can become impatient with any discussion about paintings which includes philosophical or religious overtones, "complications" as she calls them. And she can become impatient with paintings themselves when they depart too far from nature in their abstractions. The discussion she enjoys is nearly entirely technical. Though she has been told it is better in watercolor to paint the background first, it doesn't work for her, earth muddying her intricate flowers if she proceeds that way. Though she has been told not to worry about perspective, she fusses if her foxgloves are too large for her hollyhocks, her rabbits as large as elephants compared to her mushrooms. The title of one painting "Mega Rabbits," is an apology as much as a joke. Though she acknowledges her debt to Rousseau, she is more apt to be interested in any painter's treatment of a cat or bird or flower or tree than she is in the work of a particular person. It is the craft of painting rather than the aesthetics of schools that preoccupies her. She is impatient with being classed with book illustrators like Beatrix Potter or primitives like Grandma Moses, not because she is necessarily indifferent to their work but because categories of that sort don't encompass her own interests, which are eclectic.

When Elisabeth Hopkins rejects religious or philosophical interpretations of painting and is particularly amused at symbolic readings of her own, she is reserving a right to be uninhibited by intellectually minimizing theories.

Yet it is hard to approach her paintings without recognizing their religious innocence. Elisabeth Hopkins is a very well and thoughtfully educated Christian who chooses to paint the world either before the fall or after the second coming. even if some of her biblical subject matter comes historically between those two events. Knowledge, critical knowledge of the sort the apple provided for Adam and Eve, is enemy to wonder. Elisabeth Hopkins, like the Adam of her many 'naming of the beast' series, names her beasts in innocent congregation as they were conceived in the beginning or as they have been prophesied to return at the redemption of the world, lion and lamb together in the peaceable kingdom. Her snakes are her most beautiful creatures, decorated with flowers, moving through magic forests with more elegance and power than the king of beasts, who in Elisabeth Hopkins' paintings can look foolish and puzzled as well as benign.

Some of Elisabeth Hopkins' watercolors are strictly realistic exercises of particular stumps, rocks, flowers, trees. Some are clearly imaginary, sourced either in her own invention or the invention of other artists. She has few rules for keeping the worlds separate. She not only dresses real cats in bows, hats and sweaters as so many children have always done, she puts straw boaters on ducks, wristwatches on lions, tattoos cougars and elephants with flowers, teapots, ladders, and pipes. There is more whimsy than mockery in her allowing animals the same decorative use of human objects that men and women have always claimed from animals in feathers, teeth, tusks, hides and furs. Her only frankly political paintings are those in which the animals stage protest marches, carrying placards with such slogans as "Let us wear the fur coats," "Down with Zoos," and "Ban Trapping."

Only domestic animals, in particular cats, are often allowed their fallen nature, shown in arch-backed, fur-risen fury, with torn ears and lost eyes, cruising back alleys. At their picnics, though they are allowed rows of carefully arranged dead mice and fish, no birds are ever served. What as a cat owner Elisabeth Hopkins tries to prevent, she will not introduce into her paintings, "Though they can't help it, of course; it's their nature." Her children's story about cats was questioned by a sensitive editor as too sexist, jealous and violent. "But cats are," Elisabeth Hopkins protested, and her insistence on moral realism for her in no way conflicts with allowing cats distinctly human ways of perceiving the world and expressing themselves particularly in relation to their owners, referred to as, "Providers."

Elisabeth Hopkins treats people much as she does cats, grouped waiting for the ferry, at a tea party, sale or playing on the beach. She is as attentive to body stance in people as she is to the multitude of postures in cats, and she as carefully and comically dresses her people in outlandishly ordinary garb. There we all are, all right, with our hopeful vanities, bored, patient, intent, enthusiastic.

Elisabeth Hopkins' most formal paintings, her mandalas and friezes, are among her most popular. The mandalas are circles of flowers, animals and birds. Her friezes are parades of mythical beasts from unicorn to serpent or of Chinese toy animals given to her by friends and admirers over the years. One mandala was used for a card by UNICEF.

Generous to many causes from Green Peace to Amnesty International, Elisabeth Hopkins is also concerned that her watercolors are now expensive enough to be out of range of some of the people who would like to buy them. At the Bau Xi there are full-sized signed prints of her work, priced for young and old pocketbooks, and marvelous postcards of her magic forests as well as the original paintings which cast a peculiar and delightful spell over their audiences. At the last show in Toronto, the usually formal and self conscious viewers began to call to each other, "Come look at the expression on this pig's face!" One woman said, "I've bought this one for my cat. I'm sure he'll like it, aren't you?" The whole of the middle school of the National Ballet Company came, took bets on how many leaves could be counted in one painting, how many creatures from spiders to tigers could be found in another, and talked with Elisabeth Hopkins about their own art. A member of the board bought a painting to give to the school. A woman who had bought a painting called, "The Liberated Sow," was approached by a man who had bought, "The Male Chauvinist Pig" because he wanted to own the pair. Did the story end there? Admirers of Elisabeth Hopkins' painting often make friends, like the lion and the lamb, in her magic climate. They sometimes even find they are related to each other. The community Elisabeth Hopkins creates and invites through her painting more than any theory about it honors her achievement. Bring your mother. Bring your children.

A Profile

One of the reasons I am myself reluctant to play "the writer" on college campuses is that I remember my own attitude toward writers when I was in college. At Stanford, the only writer of the numbers who read and lectured at us I remember is Joyce Cary who spoke both brilliantly and helpfully about point of view. The others are simply a blur of vulnerable backs at wine and cheese parties, surrounded by aggressive and often hostile students and junior faculty, vying for attention.

Even earlier, when I was at Mills College, I remember feeling—how can I admit it?—superior to a poor young Englishman who visited our writing class on the strength of one published novel about his school days. When Anais Nin came, I had never heard of her (this was 1950). Small, stiff, and aloof with nervousness, she took to us no more than we took to her. When we were given an exercise to imitate the style of her novels, I did a parody.

Jessamyn West actually came to teach a writing course. A personable and warm woman, she shared a lot of the

practical details of being a writer, showed us her galleys
from *The New Yorker,* let us help her celebrate a sale of
poems to *The Ladies' Home Journal.* Of the writing I did
in her class, I only remember with some embarrassment
a long critique of one of her own novels as far too ham-
handed in its use of symbolism. She was obviously also a
patient and generous-spirited woman with the arrogant
young. I am an admirer of her work now, but as an untried
student I considered her involvement with popular magazines a taint to her reputation.

I didn't invent such a judgment. It was taught to me
in every one of my literature courses. Those few of the great
writers, like Shakespeare and Dickens, who were popular
in their own time had to be excused for it before we advanced to taking them seriously. The image of a great writer
was always someone obscure in *his* own time whose genius
was too advanced to flower except slowly into the cultural
consciousness. Though I found Virginia Woolf hard to read,
she was a woman; she had depended on her own press (never
referred to as vanity publishing where she was concerned);
the sale of her books was modest; she suffered bouts of
insanity and killed herself. She was a real writer.

Jessamyn West nearly died of t.b. when she was a young
woman, an experience which should have made her literarily
impeccable, but she didn't dwell on it, and she was a woman
of such cheerful and abounding energy, it was easy to forget
the mortal solitude in which she had learned her craft.

Several of us graduating together had decided that a year
in England was necessary to our development as writers.
Because Mills College is small and the faculty inclined to
parental indulgence, we were given letters of introduction
to a Scottish writer, March Cost, then living in Tunbridge
Wells. We'd never heard of her either and had no intention
of following up this opportunity to cope with yet another
"obscure," popular writer. If she had been Christopher Fry
or Dorothy Sayers (not because of her mysteries but because

of her plays and translation of Dante) or C. S. Lewis, we might have been tempted though proper timidity would surely have prevented us.

Some months went by before a letter of mild rebuke came from Mills at our failure to contact March Cost. Still we were unmoved. One of us had taken to following a drunken Dylan Thomas around London and was receiving hate mail from his wife. Another was being evaluated by Peter Ustinov. My heart already anchored, I was too busy writing a novel to take time to meet a novelist.

I was the only one of us with a phone, and therefore it was I who heard the nearly sepulchral tone announcing itself to be March Cost. Sure that one of my friends was playing just another practical joke on my easily exposed conscience—I was priggish as well as arrogant—I responded only minimally to this information and listened hard enough through an invitation for the three of us to have lunch with her on a specified date at a specified London hotel, sure I would be able to recognize the disguised voice of someone I knew. Only in the silence that followed this offer of hospitality did it occur to me that I was actually listening to March Cost and not making the proper response. In my embarrassment I then became extravagantly forthcoming, accepting for us all.

In a mood of near mutiny, my friends traveled through a drenching day in nearly forgotten finery reserved for looking like presentable daughters or granddaughters. Fortunately, we were early enough to find a ladies' room to wring out our hair, scrape the mud off our shoes, and relieve our nervous bladders. Both my companions were in cubicles, and I was standing before a full length mirror when the outer door opened. There reflected in the glass was a woman nearly my size (I was 6'2½" in my heels that noon), dressed in outlandish elegance, who could have been fifty or seventy. She posed dramatically and addressed my reflection. "Are you mine?"

Her smile was hopeful enough to suggest that I would do.

As I introduced the others, I hoped my leading role would gradually be taken over by the prettiest or the most diversely talented of us, who was not only a poet and playwright but an artist and actress as well. But the first question March Cost put to us was our birthdates. When she discovered that not only I but my mother had been born in late March, the other two had no opportunity to be more than handmaidens to the princess.

"I gave myself the name March because all my nearest and dearest were born in March."

Though I was the center of attention, I didn't have to talk much. Through drinks in the lounge and lunch in the dining room, where she chose our meals for us served by an overly attentive waiter, March Cost entertained us with the story of her life.

She had gone to art school, but for a time she was an actress in a troupe that traveled around England and Scotland, performing Shakespeare. She retreated from that into designing book jackets for a publisher who then also asked her to write copy for some of the books. When she turned that in, her employer suggested that she was really a novelist. She, therefore, retired to an 18th century cottage in Scotland to write a novel. One day, exploring the cottage, she found a portrait of herself in 18th century costume and surmised that she had been drawn to the place by that earlier incarnation of herself, whose style of dress she had since often adopted as she had today. The novel she wrote was called *A Man Named Luke* and enjoyed a remarkable success. Eleanor Roosevelt had been seen reading it on a plane. March's fortunes as a novelist had been uneven after that amazing beginning, which meant she must turn out a book every eighteen months to maintain an income she could live on.

The idea that anyone except the very famous (that is, writers I had not only heard of but read) made a living at writing was new to me and distasteful, particularly as an admitted goal. People who wrote for money were hacks.

Everyone in March's family, the Morrisons, were hacks, turning out either film scripts or historical novels, their careers inspired, March said, by her father's always providing them with lots of sharpened pencils.

The disdain I felt for that biographical detail now touches me with a tired tenderness for all of us who have to answer the same questions over and over again. Even the ones that were initially interesting finally call up in us nothing but the recorded messages on our answering service.

That March felt called upon to "be a writer" for three young Americans with nothing but preposterous ambitions to recommend us says simply that she was a kind friend to the friends who had sent us.

If it hadn't been for my birthdate, that luncheon would have been duty discharged on both sides, and indeed it was for March and the other two, who did not envy me my distinction but did take every opportunity to tease me rather as school children do a child who is pet of an unpopular teacher. I made what good jokes I could of my astrological burden, feeling only faintly guilty at such ingratitude.

March Cost was, of course, no burden. She phoned occasionally when she was to be up in London. I lunched with her. Once I went with her to a fitting of new clothes in her Scottish tartan, feeling something between a gigolo and an adopted daughter. When she was to be away in France doing research for her next book, she offered me the use of her elegant Tunbridge Wells flat to get on with my novel away from the distractions of the city. I refused. Having once been there, I knew I would be ill at ease in its formality, nervous of the antiques. When I finished my book, she offered me an introduction to her publisher, which I accepted.

Collins was not the publisher I would have chosen to submit my book to. I would have gone right to Faber and Faber, but I was oddly realistic about my accomplishment. I knew it wasn't publishable, and it was easier to be refused by a publisher I didn't much respect. When the manuscript came back, a note from a reader fluttered out of its pages, "poetic tripe by an invert." I didn't send it anywhere else.

Once I invited March to my own cold water flat in West Hampstead (not to be confused, as I had when first hearing about it, with lovely Hampstead). Some of us had decided to have a myth party, the evening's entertainment our reading of myths we had written. March accepted but declined to read anything of her own. She thought of herself, after all, as my mentor, and she sat listening rather too dramatically rapt for my comfort. That she would bestow her approval on my work was a foregone conclusion. She was too tactful to do it before the others, but she telephoned me the next day to tell me the others were clever and charming, but I was the only one who would be a real writer. I had the gift. My professors' view of my ambition was that I might be a first-rate scholar but I'd probably never be anything but a second-rate writer. I was not accustomed to flattery and neither trusted nor liked it. I had fed everyone a meal of club house sandwiches and toll house cookies, under the misapprehension all that year that offering American food would be a revelation to the English. March had found it exotic and inedible, but she complimented me on the meal, too.

I probably did invite her to visit me in the States. Such suggestions are the American equivalent of other mindless pleasantries like, "Have a nice day." She was a colorful minor player in the amazing drama of the first year I had devoted to becoming a writer, and I dined out on her as I did on my wretched brother's friends who sponged on us all, brought prostitutes into our living rooms when we wouldn't grant them our favors, or on the sight of the golden coach rehearsing in Hyde Park before the coronation.

I couldn't have been more astonished when, settled at my invalid and reclusive grandmother's house in order to do graduate work at Stanford, the phone again brought me that voice sounding from beyond the grave. In a deep, dramatic near whisper, March Cost told me that she was in San Francisco. One of her books had just become a book club selection, and she had decided to come to visit her "spirit family." She obviously expected to be invited to stay.

Grandmother, who was generous with visitors only in any investment to keep them from her door, gave me a handsome amount of money to go to San Francisco to meet March and show her the city. I explained only that she was a Scottish novelist who had been kind to me and was now in the States promoting her new book.

Then I phoned my more hospitable parents in San José, and Mother said they'd be glad to have March Cost for a week if she'd like to come.

Before I left for the city, I slipped my passport into my handbag. I didn't have a driver's license, and the waiters at the bar at the top of the Mark could be sticky if you couldn't prove you were twenty-one.

I felt smug with foresight when I was, in fact, challenged for identification. March, a contemporary highlander that day, looked bewildered at the sight of my passport and produced her own, asking, "Are we in a different country then?" The waiter had the courtesy to study hers as he had mine.

Sitting across from her high above the city, I was struck not by her outlandishness but by her beauty. It had not occurred to me before that she was beautiful. Oh, I knew she admired her own profile because photographs on her dust jackets tended to display it tilted down into a bunch of violets. (I'd remembered to buy her violets at a street stand.) Nor had I ever speculated about her personal life, about which she never spoke. I suddenly supposed it must have been tragic, and I felt both protective of her and hopeful that she might be a more presentable guest than I had feared, for though her belief in the stars, reincarnation, and second sight would not find murmuring assent in anyone I was related to, she also had an earthy humor and appetite for fun which might charm my family. The flaw in our relationship was probably my own. I was too young to know how to be charmed, a talent that can only be developed when one has outgrown embarrassment.

I got back to my grandmother's late that night, expecting to find her awake, for she had come to an age where she slept very little. I did not expect the impatient excitement of her greeting.

"Why didn't you tell me who she was?" Grandmother demanded.

"I thought I had."

"But she's *the* March Cost. Every one of my friends just waits for her next book. They're all so impressed that you know her and very envious of me that I'm going to meet her."

Grandmother had been on the phone not only to her friends but to my mother, and between them they had organized March's visit, which included stopping at Grandmother's for tea on the way down to San José. Since I had already explained my grandmother's poor health and reclusiveness to March, she would be aware of the honor, but, though Grandmother now also had a sense of being honored, I didn't count on her pleasure in the experience.

Grandmother had a defensive investment in her image. Because it had been tarnished by divorce and then marriage to an alcoholic, she had withdrawn from the social world, receiving only a few old friends who came with calling cards and white gloves to be discreetly served tea or sherry by Grandmother's devoted maid. Grandmother always sat in the same chair, backed by a wall of leatherbound books she had never read—what of the world reached her came by way of the radio—and fronted by a handsome card table, always ready for a game of solitaire, or gin rummy or coon hollow if she could find challengers.

It was there she sat to receive March Cost, who posed as dramatically for her as she had in that ladies' room for me. She gave Grandmother a blazing smile and said, "But, my dear Carlotta—I may call you Carlotta?—you are simply perfect!"

I watched my pretty little grandmother blush and fall in love. I was too relieved to be embarrassed for her, so vulnerable to such blatant flattery.

Everything about March Cost was so grand, histrionic and generous that most adults fell under her spell, amiably taking up the roles in her life which she assigned them.

Mother took me aside and explained that, since March called me Jane and Grandmother Carlotta, she couldn't call my mother either Jane as she was accustomed to or Carlotta which she had never used, and must, therefore, call her "Janetta." In the long and loving friendship they established, Mother always announced herself to March as "Janetta," answered to that name and signed all her letters with it.

By the time I arrived at my parents' house for the weekend, March had obviously made herself at home. Before dinner from the back page of the newspaper she read all our horoscopes aloud to us.

My father, who had been a navigator during the war, put down the front page and said, "March, even if there were any truth in it, the meridian established is two hundred years out of date," and put up his paper again.

"Isn't he a darling?" March crooned to my mother.

In the kitchen, Mother was full of questions. Who was the man whose picture March kept by her bed, every other day in his distinguished sixties, every other day a handsome young man? To whom did she send nearly daily telegrams, and why did she waste the money when she claimed telepathy worked just as well? How old was she, anyway? I could satisfy her curiosity about none of them.

Mother and I were taking March to Carmel for the day on Saturday. I'd already warned Mother that March found the speed on the highways terrifying, but it was difficult and sometimes dangerous to drive those roads at English country lane speed. March sat between us in the front seat. It was as if she were somehow physically attached to the accelerator. As Mother's foot went down, March's eyes closed and her body stiffened. I'd peer around that image of terror and make a face at my mother. As her foot eased up, March relaxed and opened her eyes.

Once Mother began to take off her sweater.

"But, Janetta, can you do that and drive?"

"At this speed I could get completely undressed and go to sleep," Mother replied cheerfully.

Twice that day we had to search out a telegraph office to allow March to slip off and send one of her mysterious messages, while Mother speculated wildly about her romantic life. Mother's fondness and amusement made March easier for me, and the exaggerated pleasure she took in every view, every flower, every shop was more contagious than embarrassing.

Mother bought some particularly good dried apricots and offered one to March.

"Why, they're delicious! I must get some for myself. Just the thing to purge one's guests. Don't you find they're so much more cheerful if you do?"

Every Christmas Mother sent March a large box of California dried fruit "For purging your guests." It became our suggested remedy for anyone around who was being less than agreeable.

March's friends at Mills, two ancient ladies who had lived together for years, had invited her to stay with them but, after she had been with them only a few days, she was forced to leave because she had inspired such jealousy.

"It doesn't matter," she said. "I knew I would be happy as soon as I was united with my spirit family."

It was my loving and fun-loving mother, obedient to the stars, who assured March's pleasure, and the bond between them was strong.

March's fortunes never rose so high again. As lending libraries closed down and television took over from light fiction the task of entertainment, even her careful historical research and strength of plot couldn't command much of an audience. Because she had written a biographical novel about a French actress, her work had attracted more serious attention in France than it did elsewhere, and she took real pleasure in that acknowledgment. She took her dwindling resources gallantly. For all her flamboyance, there was a strong practical side to March, who could deal firmly with publishers and was no fool about the marketplace.

I did not stay in as faithful touch with March as Mother did, partly because I had no early success to report, having been caught up in making my living as a teacher and writing only in the spare bits of time I had. It was over ten years before I wrote a novel which was published, in England by Secker and Warburg. March rejoiced at the news which vindicated her early judgment of me.

I saw her once again when I was in London. She arranged to meet me at the Ritz for tea. In that ladies' room, there were silver backed brushes and combs, but March didn't burst in to greet me. She was carefully arranged at a window table to be able to receive guests graciously without having to stand. A wig imitated her once handsome head of hair, lost to cancer treatments, but the profile remained.

She spoke to me now as a fellow writer, confessing her problems with her publisher, her pleasure in my fine firm. Her voice was weaker now, more often the voice of her phone calls. When she spoke of my book, after praising the writing, she said, "You must not stay with this subject. The world is changing but not that fast. It will not be good for your career, and you must think of that."

Though her advice was no more use to me than her praise had been, I understood the generosity of her concern. I was no longer living in the glow of adolescent ambition and arrogance. I had begun to learn how hard and often lonely it was to be a writer of whatever sort. Though the companions of my London year had worked hard and well enough each to publish a book, they had then turned away from that commitment, the standards too high, the rewards too few. March Cost had given her gallant, mysterious, flamboyant life to it with only these intermittent holiday appearances for those the stars had claimed for her. The real secret of her life was that it was private and lonely and had to be. Though the dainty sandwiches were cold and soggy, I think of our last meeting as an entirely charming hour.

The 4th of July, 1954

1954 was the last year I celebrated the 4th of July. I was not in a patriotic mood. I had been living in England when Joe McCarthy began to attract international attention with his witch hunts for communists. Six thousand miles from home, I couldn't believe anyone I knew would take such a man seriously. The press in Europe must be exaggerating and distorting the purges in Hollywood, the loyalty oaths being demanded at public universities, the general hysteria created by the UnAmerican Activities Committee hearings. After I'd been back in the States for a month, I found very few people who had not been convinced, even though they criticized some of his rough tactics, that Joe McCarthy was doing the country an essential service in ridding it of dangerous subversion. The few people who tended to agree with my European view of him as an opportunistic madman, were my college professors, whose assessments were considered suspect because of their own political vulnerability. McCarthy had convinced people that educational institutions were hot beds of communism.

I can't blame the political climate alone for how alienated I felt, for I had left in England the woman with whom I'd been living and could see no way over the financial difficulties of getting back to her and living again in that sane and nourishing country. I had written my first unpublishable novel and was facing, at the Stanford Graduate School of Writing, the unreality of my ambition to write about and as I pleased and also be published. But, when McCarthy began his investigation of the army and made it clear that he equated homosexuals with communists, his activities gave a national focus to my personal discomforts. Having no success in finding bona fide communists, he'd have little trouble locating homosexuals in all his targeted institutions, in one of which I'd have to make my living.

At the end of an entirely unproductive academic year, I was killing time until I left for a teaching job in New England in the fall, and I welcomed nearly any distraction. Alan, a law student from Harvard who had a summer job in a San Francisco law firm, was recommended to my attention by a mutual friend. He also had some ambition to write, but, as it had been with so many students at Stanford, that interest made him competitive rather than companionable. His nervous, put-down wit quickly tired me, and I could not imagine feeling comfortable in his world at Cambridge where I'd be that fall. I couldn't even pay lip service to the lie I was supposed to be learning to live in McCarthy's America.

When Jessamyn West invited me to her house in Napa to celebrate the 4th of July and to bring a friend, I proposed the outing to Alan because he was a presentable young man, had a car to drive me there, and would be impressed with meeting a successful writer.

I had never been to Napa. It was a joke rather than a place because it was the location of a large mental hospital, the funny farm, the loony bin. To make it a destination appealed to both Alan and me. For him it underlined the bizarre quality of his whole summer. At the moment he was working on a suit against the Telephone Company brought by the Pendleton Shirt Company because the "r" had been left out of a large ad in the yellow pages. For me there was gallows' humor in proceeding voluntarily to a place where some of my homosexual compatriots were already incarcerated.

We arrived in early afternoon at the appointed time. Jessamyn and her husband, the superintendent of Napa schools, had been out horseback riding, and preparations for the party had hardly begun. The local guests weren't expected for another couple of hours. I became part of Jessamyn's kitchen disorder while Alan made an impression on our host and browsed in the library. The distracted conversation between Jessamyn and me had mostly to do with what had happened to members of her writing class since we'd graduated two years before, nearly all of whom had dropped out of various independent schemes into marriage, and with the news of the Mills faculty members, who were outraged supporters of their beleaguered counterparts at the University of California, already being forced to take the loyalty oath.

The generous and casual feast was ready by the time the others arrived, three couples, the head of the mental hospital and his wife, the principal of the high school and his wife, the local undertaker and his wife. Her recent adventures dominated the opening minutes of the party. She had flown to Detroit to pick up a new hearse and had driven it back across the country, an odyssey with obvious appeal to those prominent residents of loonyville.

I was surprised and relieved to see how willingly Alan became an appreciative audience to people obviously too old to be within his range of competition. When Jessamyn took the floor, she played to the two of us much as she had to her students in class, appealing to us rather than trying to impress us.

Jessamyn was a large, robust woman, sandy-haired and freckled, looking much younger than her fifty-odd years, a headlong, hopeful, and candid woman with the energy of a horse about to bolt. Her husband, Max, seemed much older than he probably was in contrast to her, and his manner with her was affectionately indulgent.

He had just bought her a television set, still considered in those days to be a rather low-brow novelty. Jessamyn was extolling its powers to reveal the human spirit and to educate the heart. As an example, she cited an interview with a man who had invented a robot. The interviewer was clever enough to lead the man into the revelation that he was in love with his robot.

I listened to the tale of exposure with less than my usual enthusiasm for Jessamyn's perceptions. She wasn't making fun of the man or his passion. She was celebrating television's power to expose such human mysteries to a large public. It was no time to plead the vulnerability of the victim of such exposure with whom I, of course, identified. The head psychiatrist might start taking notes.

Those who did protest argued that a general audience was ill equipped for such insights and would take the vast amounts of trivia at their face value and forget how to read. It was a diabolical invention to control the masses and destroy culture.

On the contrary, Jessamyn argued. Now that the American public was having an opportunity to see McCarthy in action at the hearings, they could see for themselves what an evil man he was. Though everyone at the party shared her view of McCarthy, they did not agree with her perception of the public, who could be the more hypnotized by his rhetoric if they watched him perform.

The conversation shifted then to McCarthy's latest dealings with the army. As heads of academic institutions or responsible for mental health, these men knew they'd get little support from a general public inclined to be suspicious of such authority. But the army was a different matter. Surely McCarthy would begin to lose sympathy and credibility, never mind inspiring the wrath of generals whose fighting forces were going to be made out to be a bunch of communist fairies.

"I want justice for that man." Jessamyn said. "I want *poetic* justice."

"And what would that be?"

"Charge *him* with being a homosexual."

"Is he?" someone asked, in mildly shocked surprise.

"So rumor has it," Jessamyn said. "Obviously his little side kicks are. *Look* at them. He's been investigating a lot of other people on much less circumstantial evidence. Hoist the man on his own petard!"

"His being a homosexual, if he is, has nothing to do with it," I said. "He should be charged with the real crimes he's committing."

I held Jessamyn's eye and didn't glance at the psychiatrist.

"But don't you see? That's the poetic part of it. Get him on his own phoney morals."

"Doesn't that make us no better than he is?" I asked.

"You're arguing for making him above the law," Jessamyn said.

"I'm arguing against bad law," I said.

I was surprised to have Alan come to my aid with lawyerly competence.

"I know what's wrong with both of you," Jessamyn said. "You think I'm a matronly lady who writes about Quakers and therefore is prejudiced against homosexuals. But I'm hopelessly tolerant about love between men and women, married or not," at which Max raised tolerant eyebrows, "between men or between women. I'm the only one of you who sees the sad beauty of a man in love with a robot."

Alan argued gallantly against having such an impression of her. I was too startled by it to have a ready comment. I so envied her her accomplishments, her confidence of opinion, her experience, that it was hard for me to comprehend that she could feel threatened and wrongly judged by us because we were young. I now realize why she put so special a value on our youth. She had missed hers, fighting nearly fatal t.b. and had no idea how awkwardly needy, defensive and uncertain of ourselves we were, how fearful of being found wanting by our elders and betters.

As the party broke up, Jessamyn decided it was far too late for us to drive home. There was a guest room. Why didn't we stay the night? Alan gave me a quizzical look. Might I be persuaded to be as liberal as our hostess? Sleeping with Alan was a great deal farther than I intended to go to supply him with dining-out stories that fall in Cambridge. And I didn't owe it to Jessamyn for her upholding of her own liberated image in our eyes. If this was a test unsafe to fail, it felt to me nearly fatal to pass.

Alan was not importantly disappointed, and he entertained himself at all the other guests' expense on the long drive home, their provincial self-importance, their various foibles. And Jessamyn West, well, she was nearly indecently interested in sex for a woman her age. He proceeded to persuade himself that she had been plotting to seduce him rather than leave the job to me. Such reinventions of the evening to restore my own equilibrium were beyond me, caught between Jessamyn's confessions of total tolerance and Alan's intolerance of everyone but his young, self-conscious self. I had the uncomfortable feeling of having been forced into bed with McCarthy if not with Alan.

Jessamyn wrote me a long, affectionate letter on yellow foolscap further explaining her views of McCarthy, of the law, of love, which maintained the same views she had expressed at the party, inviting me to change mine. If I'd had the courage to answer as a homosexual, I would have made no headway in the argument. Instead I would have been excused from it, disqualified by my inability to be disinterested. I would have become for Jessamyn, like the man with his robot, an example of one of the sadder beauties of the human heart, if not a candidate for the funny farm.

McCarthy was finally defeated as he should have been

defeated, exposed as having defamed numbers of people, disrupted whole institutions without having uncovered the rampant subversion he had promised though he had uncovered and ruined the careers of numbers of homosexuals and left many other people under clouds of suspicion which didn't dissipate for years. Jessamyn didn't get her poetic justice, and homosexuals were spared the shame of having to claim him as one of us.

The political story didn't end there, however. Nixon, who had allied himself with the witch hunts, became vice president, and finally president. Because he was a cousin of Jessamyn's, I assumed he was something of a political embarrassment to her even before he was forced to resign, but in the tolerance of her heart she told of receiving a copy of his memoirs, inscribed, "To the most famous author in the family from the most infamous." And now Reagan, a leader in the Hollywood witch hunts of the 50s, looks ready for a second term of economically inspired anticommunist hysteria, pandering to all the bigotry of the far right. Those who attack him seem bent on poetic justice, too, pointing out that, though he defends prayer in the schools, he himself doesn't attend church, though he extolls the family, he doesn't see the children and grandchildren of his first marriage, while his hostility to the poor in his own country and elsewhere is given political justification. The poor, like homosexuals, are easily corruptible by communists.

The leaders in the country are much nearer now than they were in 1954 to the poetic justice of being hoist on their own petard. Perhaps, as in the ruins of Coventry Cathedral where a shard of rock exposes the carved words, "Father Forgive," a fragment of stone may read, "With Justice and Mercy for All" at the end of the final fireworks celebrating the greatest nation on earth.

I left the country, and for thirty years I have not marked the date.

"Silly Like Us," A Recollection

Wystan Auden said, "I'm a poet only when I'm writing a poem." He wrote in the early hours of the morning before the household woke. By the time he came slowly down the outside stairs that led to his farmhouse study, he was not a poet but simply a famous old man, coping with the nearly intolerable burdens of that role.

It shocks me to realize that he was only a year or two older than I am now when I met him in 1962. He was fifty-five. It was not simply that amazing ruin of a face, the skin folding in on itself, melting, but the shuffling walk caused by his outsized and painful feet, clad always in bedroom slippers. His clothes hung badly on him and were spotted with dropped food and spilled drink, dotted with small ash burns. His large, helpless hands shook. Much of his conversation was not converse at all but a prerecorded tape of anecdotes and opinions which he dutifully or irritably set in play for whoever happened to be there, old friend or stranger.

Bad habits do age, but added to the cigarettes he smoked and the daily intake of wine and gin were the drugs doctors so ignorantly prescribed back in the 50s for people of his nervous temperament who had to face the strains of public life and suffered what was then trendily called "the fight or flight syndrome." He took nightly sleeping pills on top of his heavy intake of alcohol, and every morning he countered the stupefaction of that waking with amphetamines. Only his steady discipline and natural attachment to duty allowed him to carry that ravaged nervous system and damaged heart into his sixty-sixth year. He had obviously been deathly tired for years by the strains and constrictions and demands of his life.

In 1962 I was thirty-one years old. Though I'd written three novels and a number of short stories, I had published nearly nothing, and I revealed my identity as a writer only to intimate friends not inclined to mock my fantasy life which seemed to be even more vulnerable than what is now called my "sexual preference," which in those days I wouldn't have considered any kind of bond with the man who wrote great poems addressed to "you" as a way of avoiding reference to gender. I was terrified of meeting him.

Helen Sonthoff, with whom I'd then been living for six years, was his old and good friend, and he had, therefore, invited us both for a weekend on our way back from Greece to England. Because he had last seen Helen when she was married to a man Wystan found both likeable and attractive, I felt the more inadequate, in his eyes, as her companion.

It was in part nervous apprehension that made me forget to double check our transfer of luggage at the Rome Airport. We arrived in Vienna with nothing but outsized handbags, full of things like sesame seed and honey cakes and other treasures from Greece. We hadn't even been wise enought to carry toothbrushes or a change of underwear. It made our trip across Vienna by taxi and our train journey out to Kirchstetten as easy as traveling in a dream, and my anxiety about the luggage, on which we would still be dependent for several months of travel, distracted me somewhat from the perils of our destination. Helen had long since given her word that she would not mention my interest in writing.

Auden was entranced with our lack of luggage. In fact, he was so impressed with two women traveling for months with nothing but handbags that we couldn't focus his attention on our need to do something over the weekend about finding our clothes.

Once he had settled us into a rather shabby Volkswagen, he began a long apology about the car which began with, "I'm dreadfully sorry about the bullet holes." There were, indeed, bullet holes in the upholstery of the back seat where I was sitting.

Auden had become fond of a young mechanic who looked after the car, and, instead of putting it up on blocks when he returned to New York for the winter, he lent the car to the boy, who, unused to such freedom and power, got in with a bad lot and went around the countryside, looting and shooting. The mechanic was now in jail, about which Auden felt at least partly to blame, having put such temptation in his way. Auden's own lawyer was coming out from Vienna the next day to discuss what might be done for the boy aside from sending him cigarettes and candy.

"The guilty have as much right to defense as the innocent," Auden observed grumpily.

His narrative kept his attention far more surely than did the road, over whose pot holes and ruts we bucketed at erratic speeds until we came to a muddy drive and finally into a parking space in a barn which chiefly housed animals.

I was to hear the pronouncement, "A poet should always keep animals," more than once over that weekend. Actually a refugee couple who lived on the place took care of both the creatures and Auden's house, what very little tending there was of it. He claimed the woman cleaned once a week, but a collection of mugs over the fireplace which had come with the house hadn't been dusted in years. A framed line drawing of Stravinsky on the living room wall was hardly visible through the grime, and the old floors tended to stick to one's feet. She did come in every morning to make the beds and do the dishes of the day before.

Once we had been introduced to these servants who came out of their quarters formally to meet us, we walked a muddy path beyond the barn to the house. Chester Kallman, who since his late teens had lived with Auden, was sitting in the sun, chuckling over Muriel Spark's *Memento Mori*, a book I very much admired. Not much older than I and about my size, he seemd a possible companion for me while Helen and Wystan spent the weekend renewing their friendship and reminiscing about old friends. But Helen was an old friend of Chester's, too. She had been one of his mentors in the kitchen when he was still a boy. They immediately began to make plans for joint ventures in the kitchen, including crepe suzette for dessert, which would leave Auden and me in what I now realize was a mutual and paralyzing shyness in the living room, gulping down over-large martinis, carefully stored each day in the deep freeze, chilled to a deceptive smoothness.

I was that first evening so drunk by the time we ate dinner that I remember nothing of it but Helen's decision to take the evening air by herself at the end of it, leaving me alone with the two men who were accustomed to retiring to bed right after dinner.

Chester, of a more practical turn of mind than Auden, realized that we needed not only night clothes but something other than our traveling suits and high heels to wear for walking the muddy lanes until our luggage arrived. While he went to get what he could find, Auden offered to show me to his own bedroom where we would sleep while he retreated to the single bed in the guest room. He and Chester had not shared a bed for years, a sorrow palpable in Auden even then. That evening I blamed drink for my either stumbling over a door sill while I remembered to duck my head under the low doorways or cracking my head when I remembered to step up but not to duck, but I reeled or stumbled into rooms all weekend, even sober unable to coordinate my response to the twin dangers.

"Have they towels?" Chester asked.

"There are two towels in the bathroom," Auden replied, both of which were already much used.

Chester cast his eyes to the ceiling and went off again to find clean towels for us. At his suggestion, I retreated to the bathroom, mainly to splash cold water on my dazed and daunted face, but, as fuzzy as I was, I still noticed large numbers of remedies for fleas, lice, and other complaints I'd mostly associated with slum living. By the time I came out, Helen was back and we could go dutifully to bed. It was only 9:30. We both got into old pairs of Wystan's pajamas and climbed into his high double bed which we shared with a feather bed, as much a presence as a live animal would have been. The combination of too much drink and great relief sent me into uncontrollable giggles at the circumstance of being in Wystan Auden's pajamas in Wystan Auden's bed. We were two Goldilocks in the house of the two bears, who were such an odd combination of gruff and motherly.

By the time we roused in the morning, Auden had come down from his study and was ready to face the practical requirements of the day. He did the shopping and Chester had made a long list for him.

"Butter?" he demanded. "I bought a pound of butter not three days ago. Where has it gone?"

"Most of it's on your tie," Chester replied.

We were to go with him to the village not only to look around but to use the one phone in the village for news of our missing luggage. Helen was still in her suit, but I was more comfortably clothed in a pair of Chester's trousers, his shirt and sneakers.

Because Helen spoke no word of German and I had taken a year of scientific German when I was thirteen, I had to make the phone call. (Auden didn't offer, our difficulty never becoming real to him.) The village street was like a set from a comic opera, and Auden was operatically greeted again and again with "Guten morgen, Herr Doktor, Professor!," a title which he benignly acknowledged and obviously enjoyed.

While he negotiated with the butcher, I was directed through a courtyard behind the butcher shop to a door on the opposite side which opened into a parlor. There behind framed wedding photographs on a much draped table was an old upright telephone with earpiece hanging at its side. If I hadn't intermittently lived a rural childhood, I would not have known how to use it. I gave the operator the number of the airline in Vienna in nervous, badly accented German numbers and then demanded to speak with someone who spoke English. Yes, our bags had been located in Rome and were being sent to Vienna. As soon as they arrived, probably later that day, they would be put on a train to Kirchstetten where we should alert the station master. I went back through that dream landscape, indoors merging into outdoors, shops and domestic spaces converging upon each other, to find Auden with a glass of beer, Helen with a glass of wine, each of which I declined. I still in those days liked a coke after breakfast and was determined to find and buy a six-pack to take back with me, even if I had to confess such a gross southern American vice to my hosts. Auden was not shocked by the habit, but I was given a firm lecture on my bad manners at buying for myself what he would expect to provide for me. I felt more cherished than rebuked and began to believe I could get through the weekend well enough by playing a six-year-old child indulged in occasional treats.

By the time we got home, Helen was needed in the kitchen to help Chester prepare an elaborate lunch for the lawyer, and Wystan and I were again left in the living room alone together.

"She hasn't changed," he said to me in some displeasure. "She hasn't changed *at all*."

Then we both hastily retreated into books.

Once the lawyer arrived, the language spoken was German of which I understood very little, Helen nothing at all. Our silence soon made itself apparent to that sensitive and civil man who suggested to Wystan that the ladies might not speak German, in which case he would be glad to speak English. Wystan replied in German as clipped and mumbled as his English that Helen had been married to a German and, therefore, of course understood it. Whether I understood or not was obviously of no great importance. Occasionally through lunch the lawyer addressed a question in excellent English to one or the other of us, but Wystan's irritation was so obvious that we three exchanged rueful smiles and gave up any further communication. After lunch Chester put on a new record, obviously comic and probably bawdy, which I doubt the lawyer could have enjoyed without the certainty that we didn't understand it. I found the afternoon oddly peaceful. Helen, for whom Wystan had once been a good and thoughtful friend, was troubled by what amounted to dismissive rudeness.

But that evening over drinks (which I treated very sparingly) and dinner, when English became again acceptable, Wystan redeemed himself in a long series of anecdotes about his stay as a visiting professor at Oxford, mostly to do with renewing old undergraduate friendships. He remembered, for instance, a young man whose only discernible talent had been a good imitation of Queen Mary, which Wystan and others decided to put to the test. They hired a Daimler, dressed one of their number as a chauffeur and took their Queen Mary to the one residence they knew where the Queen was occasionally received. When the butler opened the door, he fainted, for the real Queen Mary was at that moment taking tea in the garden. Reminiscing about similar exploits, Wystan and Lord David Cecil, among others, competed to remember the worst gaffe of their undergraduate days. Cecil described being invited for a weekend to the country house of a friend where the chief entertainment was hunting. Having never before held a gun in his hands—and what nearly spastic hands they were when I watched him lecture at Oxford—he took up the weapon, fired and felled his host's father. Though I wanted to ask how badly the man had been wounded, the story ended instead only with the horror that it had happened on Friday, leaving Cecil to live through the whole weekend in embarrassment.

Our safely hilarious meal ended with Wystan's insisting, against Chester's firm warning, on trying the sesame and honey cake we'd brought from Greece. He took one bite, and his full set of false teeth came out of his mouth imbedded in the cake. Toothless, he swore at the incompetence of Chester's father, who was Wystan's dentist. The Greeks also came in for their share of abuse. For the rest of the weekend, Wystan complained of coming upon stray sesame seeds.

Helen invited herself to church with Wystan the next morning, a Catholic church which was good enough for the Anglo-Catholic Auden, and they obviously enjoyed themselves singing heartily and stopping for a drink on the way home, which must have given them time to speak of Helen's husband and other old friends who had inhabited Helen's life before I met her.

Chester and I spent a companionable enough morning, mostly at separate occupations. He seemed to me perched rather than settled in his life there, most of his rude observations expressing a rough affection for Wystan, but there was an edge to them, too, as if he felt bound to an irritating old man who also happened to be a giant the world worshipped, which explained the deep contradiction of Chester's indifference and fierce jealousy.

Wystan tried to correct the imbalances in their relationship. He rarely mentioned his own work but talked freely of Chester's. We listened to a broadcast of an opera for which Chester had written the libretto. But once Wystan's attention strayed from Chester, he was apt to pontificate on the church, on the monarchy, and he seemed to me nearly perversely conservative in his harsh judgment of a niece who had married beneath her. Only when he commented on other people's writing was he, on principle, generous, but he was neither very thoughtful nor very interesting, a tired man filling the empty social space for lack of energy to listen. As a younger man, Helen says, he was a very good listener, a habit he may have intentionally broken after it had often involved him too intensely in other people's lives.

No man of our time has written more insightfully about love. I don't know how many of the love poems are to Chester, but somewhere under that old, fuddling voice, there was the voice of the poet calling, "Dear flesh, dear mind, dear spirit. O dear love," posing questions, "To settle in this village of the heart,/ My darling, can you bear it?" making confessions, "There are not fortunes to be told, although / Because I love you more than I can say, / If I could tell you I would let you know." But the fair, brooding face didn't any longer hear it. Auden has been eloquent, too, about such loss. I do not think it would have comforted him at all to know that Chester didn't long outlive him, died in Athens of an overdose of drugs at the age of fifty.

Wystan's chief concern on the morning of our departure was the amount of money we should tip his help, a figure that was arrived at by doubling the amount they could reasonably expect of anyone but Americans, which Helen and I at that time still were. He supervised my counting out of the bills before putting them into the envelope he provided. I think it annoyed him that I, rather than Helen, handled the money. The couple were there at the barn, waiting to say good-by. Feeling both bullied and amused, I handed over the money.

Our suitcases didn't arrive until minutes before we were to board our train back to Vienna, just in time to claim them with their tags, "Herr Rule c/o W. H. Auben," one of which I saved for its comic inaccuracies so accurately reflecting the uncertain communications of the weekend which, nevertheless, got the bags to their destination.

In writing "In Memory of W. B. Yeats," whom Wystan thought "a prize son of a bitch," he was also speaking of himself: "You were silly like us: your gift survived it all."

Time "Worships language and forgives
Everyone by whom it lives;
Pardons cowardice, conceit
Lays its honors at their feet."

I am comforted to know that he is right. I left Kirchstetten frightened for rather than of Wystan Auden, growing harder to care for as he needed more care, hauling his baggage of fame which grew heavier with each passing day.

Now ten years after his death, honors are being laid not at those real and painful feet of clay, but at the surviving gift left by a man "silly like us" whose spirit nevertheless rose each morning in that dying flesh to make him once again, each unique moment, a poet.

PART IV:

REFLECTIONS

The Cutting of Pages

My great-grandmother, Jane Vance, for whom I am named, had three complete sets of Dickens. My grandmother, Carlotta, inherited the pink set, which was placed among other handsomely bound complete collections of other writers ranging from Mark Twain to Conrad and Balzac on a bookcase behind the chair in which she always sat. I was in my teens before I discovered that most of the pages of the Dickens had never been cut.

"It was Oma's best set," my mother explained.

When, in my turn, I placed the Dickens on my own shelves, I vowed, though Dickens is not among my favorite writers, to cut the pages and read every one of the thirty volumes, either as a duty to literature or a cover-up for my non-reading grandmother. I may not live that long because it is not on my list of compulsive activities. Also the space those books take on my shelves is a daily rebuke to my own about-to-be ten volumes, testimony to modest ambition and too easily distracted industry.

I did meet my great-grandmother on my first trip west from New Jersey to spend some weeks in the California

217

redwoods. I was only sixteen months old; so I don't remember her, the proof of the meeting only in the old photographs of the four generations, I standing wispy-haired and squinting by my great-grandmother's knee. She sits heavily, solidly in a garden chair out under the trees at Carlotta, the summer place named for my grandmother. Her face is passive, as it is in every photograph I've seen of her, though in one there is a liquid expression of eye hard to read, sad perhaps but maybe simply absent from the experience of being photographed. It is a broad planed, regularly featured face, handsome rather than pretty.

My mother loved and was loved by Jane Vance, who kept her granddaughter for every school holiday.

"She never played with me," my mother says, "but she let me do everything she did."

When as a child I occasionally stayed at Carlotta with my spinster great aunt, Etta, my days were very much what my mother's had been, and I was never lonely or bored. There were always chores to be done in the large flower gardens. The roses which surrounded the house were always referred to as Jane Vance's garden though she had been dead for some years. The acre of formal gardens behind the house was Etta's. The maids in the kitchen always needed to be supplied with wild berries or fruit from the orchard or vegetables from the garden down the hill on the flat by the barns.

Etta herself made the fancier salads and cakes. There was the frosting bowl to lick, the cheesecloth to hold for making the cottage cheese from the large pans of milk left on the back of the wood stove.

Every evening but Sunday, there were card games, and quilting and embroidery were always at hand. I learned to replace the cylinders and crank up the victrola. We listened to Harry Lauder, to dance tunes of around the turn of the century. The pink Dickens also was published in 1900.

In the attic at Carlotta, there were elegant old hats, traveling dusters, party dresses, as well as stacks of old magazines. I have now a bound volume of copies of *Godey's Ladies' Book.* The magazines were too old-fashioned to hold my attention for long, and the clothes were all far too small for me to try on. In the family Etta was considered tall, but I'd taken real height from my father's family. The Vances seemed to me a diminutive bunch.

I was not, in my childhood, particularly curious about the woman for whom I was named. Only after my grandmother died and I was given things I had thought of as hers did my mother remind me that they'd first, like the Dickens, belonged to Jane Vance. For Mother they came to me as the right of the namesake from a woman she had loved far more easily and fully than she had her own mother.

The pottery presentation piece, a lidded jardiniere which had stood in the curve of my grandmother's grand piano, I claimed only because, when I was staying with her during a brief stint of graduate school, I once stowed cold cans of beer in it for entertaining my own friends. My name for it was "The beer cooler." But Mother told me it had been presented to Jane Vance by Josiah Wedgewood, on what occasion for what reason she did not know.

I did not think of my great-grandmother as a society woman, entertaining visiting notables, but obviously, before my great-grandfather, John Vance, died (before my mother was born) she did. He was president of a bank and a railroad and owned a lot of town property in Eureka as well as stretches of redwoods and farm land in the surrounding countryside.

There were also parties for the young people, three daughters and a son, a private train ordered to take them and their friends from Eureka to Carlotta for weekends. But it was not entertaining for the purpose of marrying them off. Jane and John Vance must have been possessive of their children, for only my grandmother, who was the youngest and her father's favorite, married before he died, and she felt guilty all her life for having left him.

Jane Vance was ten years younger than her husband.

They met for the first time when she was ten and he was twenty. He had gone back for a visit to Nova Scotia and called at the house in which he'd been born. The child who had also been born there fixed in his imagination, and six years later he returned to claim her and take her to California.

Her children remembered her as a timid and fearful woman, protesting against her husband's love of fast horses, hanging charms and potions around the necks of her children, teaching them respect for every superstition. But once her husband was dead, she was afraid of nothing, "as if her life didn't matter after that," my grandmother explained.

Yet after she was a widow, she was the central warmth of my mother's childhood.

In my favorite photograph of her, she's standing in a rowboat in a full length dress, a hat, a fishing rod in one hand, trout or perhaps steelhead in the other. Mother says she went on fishing even when she had to be carried into the boat. She was a famous fisherwoman, designed and tied all her own flies, wrapped her own rods, one of which is out in my garage. Maybe she took Josiah Wedgewood fishing.

Often she went alone, and, when her catch was larger than her family's appetite, she'd trade it for Indian baskets at the Hoopa encampments along the river. In my childhood those baskets hung on the redwood walls of our cabin by the south fork of the Eel River, a place used only as a fishing camp in Jane Vance's day. Now they hang on the cedar walls of my own house, winnowing baskets, storage baskets, hats, encased bottles in intricate abstract designs and subtle colors. Perhaps I think of her as a gardener and fisherwoman and collector of Indian baskets because I am more familiar with what was her summer life at Carlotta which she shared with my mother rather than her winter life in the large house in the little city of Eureka. I went to that house several times as a child. My mother's doll collection was still kept in a bedroom that was thought of as hers. Aunt Etta showed me her own hope chest, full of fine work, at the foot of her chaste bed. It is now full of sweaters in my downstairs hall. Jane Vance's birds and her aviary had long since gone, as had Etta's parrot, the taunter of my mother's childhood. I climbed to the attic which had once been a ballroom, now full of trunks, boxes, furniture, dress frames, and there was a turret window where Jane Vance sat looking out over the city to the harbor watching for a ship to pass safely over the dangerous sandbar, bringing her daughters home from boarding school in San Francisco, Ida, Etta, and Carlotta.

Ida, the prettiest and most light hearted of them, died in childbirth. Etta chose not to marry. She had a wealth of wooing jewelry—I wear one of the sapphire and diamond bracelets—to prove it was by choice that she stayed home with her mother. Carlotta, my grandmother, divorced when Mother was four and remarried in haste and unhappily. The one son, Harry, was a diabetic and went blind at twenty-one. He married and had two children, younger than my mother. The family did not like his wife. They cosseted him.

What did Jane Vance make of her family, I wonder now. She must have grieved bitterly for her firstborn and love-liest child. She bought her son-in-law out of his share of family property, and afterward he felt cheated by her. She was afraid he might kidnap my mother and hold her for ransom. The blindness of her only son was so hard a fact that no one in the family was ever allowed to refer to it. According to Mother, who never liked Etta, she and her mother quarrelled a lot. Etta didn't stay at home to be a comfort to her mother but because she liked her own comfort too well. And the youngest, my grandmother, who hated Eureka once she'd tasted San Francisco, married the first man who promised to take her away, and sent her child home for holidays.

"I hated to go home," my grandmother said. "Mother would begin to cry the evening of the first day because already one day had gone."

Jane Vance taught my young father to fish, a sport he's

enjoyed all his life, and her example must have been at least one of the reasons he indulged me in my wish to go fishing or hunting or wherever the men were going rather than to stay behind with the women. It was the wonderful picnic lunch and the adventure out of doors rather than the sport which enticed me.

At home in the summer, whether at Carlotta or at our cabin by the Eel, the women gardened and cooked and preserved, in the evening did handwork, played cards, and remembered. I would have liked the stories more if they'd been less nostalgic. The wistfulness Etta, Harry, and Carlotta all had for the great days of their childhood and youth diminished a present I wanted to be as mythic for me as their past had been for them. But the place where they had all danced was a dusty attic, and the aviary was empty of bright birds. The journey from the Eel to Carlotta by car was swift and sick-making rather than long and dangerous, rivers to be forded by buckboard, Indians not always friendly. And there was no private train anymore, filled with excited young people, of whom only Ida was real to me, having stayed young in her siblings' imaginations.

All my childhood, I had the feeling that I was expected to grow up into a world that no longer existed, Jane Vance's world as she offered it to her children before death, blindness and misery overcame them.

But she had touched my mother in a different way, given her a model of grandmotherliness from which her own grandchildren benefit. In her memory now, Mother would skip that sad, failed generation to have us know Jane Vance is source. They are things which have been handed down to us, talismen charged not with a failed world but with her abiding love of that child, my mother.

I have Jane Vance's beautiful ivory and bamboo Mahjong set, a game she played on Sunday when cards were forbidden. She apparently had no knowledge of its heathen history. I have never learned to play the game, not having carried the amusement of games past childhood, but I did once read the rule book and study the symbols, the winds and dragons, in order to write a scene in a novel of four old people playing that game. In the same novel I sent a character up to the attic where Jane Vance once watched for ships.

Since neither she nor the world she lived in were there for my growing up, I have had to learn my own uses for the things passed down to me for making a world of my own. I can't imagine that she would feel at home in it, but she has made me feel more at home living in Canada where she was born, with the baskets and the beer cooler, cutting my way through the pink set of Dickens.

Funny People

"When the people on this ferry stop looking funny to you, you'll know you've lived on your island too long," my mother said.

I had, even then, to look around to see what she meant, for, because I'd taught at the university through generations of various rebellions against convention, "funny looking people" for her were my norm. Long-haired men in embroidered denim shirts, ragged jeans and work boots, long-haired women in floor-length skirts and sandals, children in a patchwork of thrift shop finds, kept warm by hand knitted ponchos of a variety of wools were the settled generation of the 60s dropouts, eking out a living on subsistence farming, selling eggs and firewood, the women also working in the local stores, the men as day laborers, paid by only modestly more affluent people living on pensions. The pensioners tended to dress up for the ferry trip to the mainland and town, but their good suits, overcoats and shoes dated back to before their retirement. They weren't shabby so much as out of date, and nearly all of them, from years of island living, wore a "funny" knitted cap or scarf, carried a woven or worked leather bag. Just the age mix, the young, the very young, and the old with only a very few representatives of those striving years between forty and sixty-five might look odd to Mother, but she does incline to think of any crowd in a public place, if it is not the symphony, as "the great unwashed."

It may have been unconsciously perverse of me to find my "funny people" just where she would feel at home at the chamber music concerts I attended when I still lived in town. That audience so fascinated and amused me that I always wanted to be there half an hour early. People conscious and confident of their appearance as important in the passing show have always attracted my attention.

There would be no chamber music concerts in the provincial outposts of North America without the strong influence and support of European immigrants. In the early 60s many of them were refugees, by then already restored to their previous professional affluence and therefore the core of "friends of chamber music," not only as subscribers but as donors and entertainers of the visiting musicians. They were an aging and prematurely aged group, afflicted with all manner of infirmities against which their high good humor and appetite for display seemed more signs of courage than vanity. Their jewels were real, as were their mangy fur coats, whose linings must once have concealed those jewels, whose missing fur had perhaps been left on the barbs of wire fencing at one frontier or another. The women tended to be much larger than the men as if women exercised their appetite for life more directly, and they were more sociable, too, pausing each two or three difficult-to-navigate steps down the aisle to look up and over their bifocals to spot a friend, wave gaily, hoo-hoo, and then carry on again. The men tended more to bow to aisleside friends. The whole ritual of arrival was made easier by the fact that, though there were no officially assigned seats, subscribers claimed their own and always sat in them. What a number of shocked looks were exchanged if an unknowing one-nighter sat in the wrong place! Only a very few of the oldest men slept through parts of the concert.

Of the other quite substantial group, the gay men of the community, there were more sleepers, for more of them came only for the purpose of arrival and for the sedate cruising at intermission or the displaying of a new pretty young conquest. After the required brief critical comment on the program or the performance, conversation moved quickly on to the success of someone's new toupee, an up-coming dinner party, the unexplained absence of one of a couple.

On a bus, ferry, or plane it can be assumed that the large majority of people share a simple, common purpose of getting across town, across the water or across a conti-nent. No concert hall or theatre could survive serving only those who came to hear the concert or see the play. Those which flourish do so by providing groups of people their opportunity to display themselves among their peers or betters.

Perhaps public transport would not have to be so heavily subsidized if it could be taken up for its less utilitarian purposes. To my knowledge only religious fanatics and drunks travel past their own stops. And tourists. In season, the Gulf Island ferries do attract their share of those.

I'm not sure why I feel protective of my fellow islanders under my mother's amused and critical regard while I felt perfectly comfortable entertaining myself with a concert audience and have no inhibitions about tourists either, among whom Mother could also be counted to feel at home, wearing the latest good looking walking shoes and raincoat, accompanied by my father slung about with all the most up-to-date camera equipment, for which by now the Japanese tourist is the best model.

It would be inaccurate to say that my parents look funny to me on the ferry. They are my parents, and I assume they respond in a similar way to me, though I know they have wished, at one time or another, that each of their children moved more completely camouflaged in their world, as I occasionally want to hide their Lincoln Continental in mine.

Some years after I'd begun going to concerts, I found myself much more often chatting with friends than people-watching. In fact, the audience as audience seemed far less interesting to me. That hoo-hooing woman, that man with the toupee now had names and particular histories for me. I was among friends.

I don't know if the people on the ferry look any less peculiar to my mother now that she's made the crossing so often herself. Perhaps one of the reasons I chose to live on the island was my almost immediate sense of comfort among its inhabitants, and for me by now there are no characters among the passengers, simply many friends, until the tourist season begins again.

There is nothing wrong with being a tourist, nothing uncomfortable about it if you are insensitive to how funny you look to the natives and simply enjoy how funny they look to you. But I think my mother is wrong about the signal to move on. When nobody looks funny to you any more, you are at home.

Ashes, Ashes

Americans take vacations. The English and Canadians take holidays. With my half-breed vocabulary I vacillate between words for our yearly trip to the south to visit relatives happily located on the Arizona desert and on the California coast. We certainly vacate the north, and we are called 'snow birds' by those who are at home picking their breakfast off the trees. Yet, because we visit family, we are there for holidays, to give our sisters plants on Valentine's Day, to celebrate birthdays, to be assaulted by flags on Presidents' Day. Strictly speaking, I suppose none of these is a holiday, except in the pagan sense. "Pagan" comes from a word meaning civilian, that is, someone who is not a soldier of Christ. We are not soldiers of Christ.

Our Arizona sisters are, and so are our closest friends there who come to lunch on Ash Wednesday, their foreheads smudged with ash crosses. I suffer a pious embarrassment, for in my churched childhood only Catholics were marked by the day, protestants rejecting such "unseemly show." Our mothers would have said, "No Popishness." But we are too polite and so are they to discuss religion now that we don't share it. As we carry on our Christless conversation, I wonder what authority may bang on the door and who of us will be taken off, the marked or the unmarked.

I turn to a friend I haven't seen since last year, tempted to ask what she has done to be penitent about, for not even that aggressive black mark can distract me from the innocence of her aging, cheerful face. She must have worn that jaunty madras jacket and those white trousers to church. My question is blandly general instead, but I am able to meet her eyes.

After a modest hesitation, she says, well, aside from work (she is a nurse in an alcohol abuse center) she is learning to be a clown. She has taken a course in which each student must discover her own persona, out of which will develop costume, make-up, and a routine. She has discovered that her persona is a child named Hugamy. Her make-up is a red heart on one cheek, an upside down heart on the other. Her costume is decorated with hearts.

"You could ask me to your birthday party, for instance," she says. "I've already done birthday parties."

"Do you talk or are you a silent clown?"

"Mostly I don't speak."

She has also gone to a week-end meeting on the healing power of laughter where Hugamy flourished.

"We have a clown on our island," I say. "He plays a tin whistle to the eagles, and he's found a clown woman. They're having a baby."

"Does he wear a costume?"

"Sometimes, and he carries red heart stickers and gives them to people on the ferry."

"How does he make a living?"

"He's a music therapist for sick children at a hospital."

"I will sometimes be Hugamy at the center."

North American Indian clowns are healers.

Our sisters come home for dinner, their foreheads fingered with ashes. One wears her cross like a blessing, the other like a brand. I want neither smugness nor guilt at the table, but they do not wash their faces.

"My husband was just as lonely when we were married as he is now, but the kids say to me, 'He's so lonely now.' and our minister says that marriage is for life. I did the right thing. I'd never go back to him. But I'm a second-class citizen."

"Oh, they don't mean that. He doesn't mean that," our widowed sister replies.

"Yes, they do. They want us back together again. Yes, he does, and you do too. You're always making remarks about people who divorce."

"Well, I don't mean it," our widowed sister answers.

"I shouldn't have married him. That's what I shouldn't have done."

Our widowed sister is the only one of us really acceptable in the eyes of the church, and she does want credit for it, having earned it in her long, hard marriage, but not really at our expense. It just happens to be that way.

Ash Wednesday wasn't put on the church calendar until 700 A.D. to make Lent forty days long (Sundays don't count) to correspond with Christ's fasting in the desert.

We are still eating Valentine's candy and cookies, all of us.

The area around Phoenix is not properly a desert. It was a valley of cotton fields until retirement compounds turned it into concrete with walled oases of planted palm, olive, orange, lemon, camellia, and gardenia. The water smells of chlorine, as it does also in Los Angeles.

We arrive there for a younger sister's birthday. Our divorcing nephew drives up from San Diego for the celebration. Having forgotten a present, he searches Glendale for a florist open after six. Finally he buys carnations at the hospital.

"Be careful the card doesn't say 'Get well soon.' "

"There's no cure for being 44."

"He ought to be driving a truck. He ought to be barefoot and wearing jeans," our sister says. "I can't get used to these three-piece suits, the Mercedes."

"The car is borrowed. We get older."

"I'm not getting involved about this divorce," she says. "It's none of my business."

His mother is trying to convince him that he's making a terrible mistake. He has a two-year-old daughter. His aunts are either silent or defend his right to do what is best for him. He is very polite to everyone, even his wife and child when he sees them. He sees himself as a statistic: a baby, a job change, a major move, any one of them can break up a marriage. They have experienced all three. His mother views it more personally.

We sisters go to a museum to see a collection of Indian art, tools for killing and cooking, masks for war and for fertility.

By the sand paintings there is a sign which explains that these are not meant to be preserved. They are healing ceremonies to restore harmony between the patient and nature, left to blow away when their task is accomplished. We are looking at the petrified medicine of clowns.

There is a special exhibit of santos, Indian depictions of the saints, of Mary and the crucified Christ. One carving has a curious perspective. While an ox is driven by an angel in human proportion to the ox, a farmer, three times their size, kneels in prayer.

"A self portrait," our sister says dismissively.

She likes best the realistic small three-dimensional worlds built by the museum staff to depict the domestic, ritual, and hunting lives of the Indians, the little toys with which we played war with our brothers when we were children before the real wars of estrangement.

(Our Arizona sisters say of a brother, "He's a peculiar man, at his best at funerals.")

I look into our sister's house that night as a domestic peep show, her youngest daughter doing algebra with her boyfriend in her darkened bedroom, her middle daughter playing tug of war with the dog by the television set. A husband sits tiredly waiting for a meal or a change of plan. We three women are variously distributed at the ironing board, dishwasher, oven, sisters doing each other's work: Southern California, circa late 20th century.

But I have become a giant farmer on his knees.

There is a storm in the night, thunder mudsliding down the hills, wind breaking the rain in waves against the house. We pitch in our beds, passengers of weather, being carried into day.

The Queen of England has also been pitched upon these shores. She and Prince Philip, the President and Mrs. Reagan are on holiday for the American people. When we are not out in the weather ourselves, playing chicken with tornado, earthquake, mud slide and flood, we watch the royal couple and our genial host and hostess on tv, under umbrellas, climbing in and out of four-wheel-drive vehicles. Occasionally we are allowed in out of the rain with the Queen to watch her remarkably private face on public show at banquet or gala.

I wonder if she's ever ironed a blouse for Princess Margaret or made peanut butter sandwiches for her niece and nephew. I know she and Princess Margaret are sisters like our sisters, the blessed and the branded, and I know they have had more than one conversation about divorce.

As we fly up the coast over catastrophic weather, we are tired of the Queen's route, not simply because she has jinxed the weather but because she has invaded our lives. Mother reads the paper each morning for details of the Queen's dress and day, for the guest lists at San Francisco luncheons and dinners which occasionally include friends of Mother's. The Queen even competes with the new football league games for Dad's attention, and the rain continues to fall. Out in it, we can't any longer escape her, for police line the route to the shopping center while crowds wait for a glimpse of her endlessly discussed hat.

One good travel tip she does offer: she carries her own drinking water.

> San Francisco garbage dumped into the Bay
> You drink for lunch in San José

It is hard to catch flickers of childhood from the corner of an eye when the creek is flooded and the streets are tattered with banners. I wonder if the Queen, off to Yosemite now, will finally get a good view of her own. I'm glad we aren't following her there.

"Why aren't they thinking of the child?" Mother asks.

"Decisions aren't ever made for the sake of the children. Their parents divorced. Your parents divorced."

"But does it have to go on and on?"

"Life does. You have a great-granddaughter."

And we are to visit her and her mother, who is late to pick us up, apologetic and hung over.

The two-year-old does not remember us. It's been a year since she's seen us, and she has other relatives now, her mother's brother and sister, cousins, grandparents. She is dignified, watchful, until we become laps and voices reading stories: the grown-up as talking chair. Our favorite image in Arizona Indian art is the storyteller, a sitting figure with open mouth, hung about with children.

"I don't know . . ." is the way her mother ends most of her comments, whether about divorcing, buying a house or getting a job. She does know. The knowledge temporarily unnerves her. She has lived half her young life with our nephew.

"Why don't you sing your ABC song?" she asks the child.

Then "Why don't we go see this house?"

Then "Why don't we take a walk?"

Keep moving, relieve the tension, the attention.

The child rides in a small red wagon, out of which she gets any time she sees something that can be circled. Then

234

at a drunken half run, around she goes, a tree, a pool, a garbage can, singing:

> Ring around the rosie
> Pocket full of posie
> Ashes, ashes
> All fall down

It is a rhyme perfectly timed for her balance since she is nearly always into a dizzy stumbling at its end, her mother reaching out to lift her away from the fall.

The first three times, it is a pretty exercise of excited baby, pursued by a laughing, singing mother, but the ritual becomes obsessive, repeating every few yards until her mother is tired, wanting to stop the game. It goes on and on into a war of wills, baby a berserk clown to whom her mother is nearly helplessly attached.

> Ring around the rosie
> Pocket full of posie
> Ashes, ashes
> All fall down

Baby is lifted screaming from the last tumble and finally subsides in a long grizzle as she's dragged back to their apartment.

We meet the young woman who lives across the hall.

"That's Peggy," the child repeats as she pulls her own wagon in through the door. "My babysitter. Sometimes I cry."

"Ashes, ashes." Is it an ancient Lenten song?

No, and that line is an American corruption of the sound of a repeated English sneeze. Even the first line, which has sent so many children round in circles, is a corruption of "Ring a ring a rosie," perhaps describing the bright rash of the plague, and "Pocket full of posie" may be the bag of herbs carried to ward off the infection, the sneezing a further symptom of a disease that wiped out whole cities, "All fall down." The medieval clowns at their healing?

The day we come home it is still raining but not because the Queen has arrived in Victoria; it is our own familiar weather. We meet a child on the road on horseback, "She looks just the same as in the olden days," she reports solemnly. On the late news, the Queen is receiving flowers from children in a park filled with instant daffodils. We are more her subjects than she is ours, now that we are back in Canada.

We have bought a lambskin home to give to our clown man and clown woman for their baby, who will also, no doubt, sometimes cry.

You Cannot Judge a Pumpkin's Happiness by the Smile Upon It's Face

Some days I give up fiction. The Memorial Society has just sent notice of its annual meeting to discuss a proposal to sponsor cheap charter flights. "Your board is of mixed emotions about this." I imagine the brochure: "Low cost adventure along with low cost death." "Try a warmer climate." "Getting there is half the fun." Would members of a memorial society be more or less nervous on take-off? To admit the problem of one day having to dispose of one's body doesn't necessarily make one sanguine about death. The date of the meeting is October 31st. Hallowe'en. Take the pomp out of the circumstance, and the spooks come cartwheeling in, trick or treating for can't-take-it-with-you trips abroad. "On the other hand we do not want to get involved in any activity which distracts from our basic purpose." Which is to bury ourselves. "Perhaps the time has come to make a tasteful, educational film on the subject . . ." Followed by some travel shorts? No, the travel shorts should come first. I haven't a mask or a Unicef can, and anyway I like to stay home on Hallowe'en, not just to protect my property; I like handing out candy to kids who have no idea they're playing dead.

When we were kids, my father made us skeleton cos- tumes with paint that glowed in the dark. He had a text- book to get it right, a girl's skeleton for me, a boy's for my brother. I didn't know the significance of walking around in the correct bones. I had only to undress to put my skeleton away, and I would have outgrown it by the next year.

"We are an organization that believes there is something basically barbaric and wrong about honouring our dead with a ceremony that places so much emphasis on the elaborate display of the physical remains."

My mother thought there was something barbaric and wrong about elaborate displays of physical presence, whether in pain or pleasure. Writhing and wriggling brought the same quiet reprimand. One should be at least as prudish and frugal about one's body when it's dead.

I did not see the basic connection between my sex and death when it might naturally have occurred to me at the first sight of my menstrual blood. I was allowed to call it 'the curse' but not allowed to curse it. I was to see it rather as the mark of potential and dangerous miracle: life. When my brother bled from the head and fainted, no one was happy for him.

Five years later, in unrelated studies of the flat worm and 17th century erotic poetry, I came upon the truth. As I cut those pointed-headed, cross-eyed worms in half, I was not committing murder but assisting in reproduction. Only the sexed creature must die. Death in those poems is a metaphor for orgasm because sex is mortality. The blood my body offers up may be for life but not for my life. It is a conspiracy against me in favor of any stranger.

Sanguine about death? Bloody-minded! I mistrust machines, flying or otherwise, because this basic machine, my body, is designed to kill me. All its appetites are suicidal. But abstinence is, too. Eating to death and starving to death are the same choice. One may take longer than the other. One may die of childbearing or of the diseases of not breeding.

"For any woman who engages in sex early, particularly with a number of partners . . ." there is another equally ordinary cancer.

Men die of overexertion, in bed or out of it.

There is no satisfactory way to rebel.

"There is a better way . . . the memorial society way."

On Hallowe'en, voting on charter flights.

Or the way it was for that group of friends in Concord. They got together in someone's shop to build their own coffins, rich people, every one, determined not to take one cent more than was necessary with them into their graves. And they were careful not to start drinking until all those electric tools were put away.

"We shall appreciate your comments."

How do they know, ahead of time? It's hilarious, all those cheap holidays, educational films, Hallowe'en parties. But the simple, dignified funeral I've signed up for is the real punch line of the long wriggling, writhing joke of life. Stop bleeding. Don't glow in the dark.

The Harvest, the Kill

I live among vegetarians of various persuasions and moral neat eaters; therefore when I have guests for dinner, I pay rather more attention to the nature of food than I would, left to my own imagination.

The vegetarians who don't eat meat because they believe it to be polluted with cancer-causing hormones or because they identify their sensitive digestive tracts with herbivore ancestors are just cautious folk similar to those who cross the street only at the corner with perhaps a hint of the superstition found in those who don't walk under ladders. They are simply taking special care of their lives without further moral deliberation.

Those who don't eat meat because they don't approve of killing aren't as easy for me to understand. Yesterday, as I pried live scallops from their beautiful, fragile shells and saw them still pulsing in the bowl, ready to cook for friends for whom food from the sea is acceptable, it felt to me no less absolute an act of killing than chopping off the head of a chicken. But I also know in the vegetable garden that I rip carrots untimely from their row. The

239

fact that they don't twitch or run around without their heads doesn't make them less alive. Like me, they have grown from seed and have their own natural life span which I have interrupted. It is hard for me to be hierarchical about the aliveness of living things.

There are two vegetarian arguments that bear some guilty weight for me. The first is the number of acres it takes to feed beef cattle as compared to the number of acres it takes to feed vegetarians. If there ever were a large plan to change our basic agriculture in order to feed everyone more equally, I would support it and give up eating beef, but until then my not eating beef is of no more help than my eating my childhood dinner was to the starving Armenians. The second is mistreatment of animals raised for slaughter. To eat what has not been a free-ranging animal is to condone the abuse of animals. Again, given the opportunity to support laws for more humane treatment of the creatures we eventually eat, I would do so, but I probably wouldn't go so far as to approve of chickens so happy in life that they were tough for my table.

The moral meat eaters are those who believe that we shouldn't eat what we haven't killed ourselves, either gone to the trouble of stalking it down or raising it, so that we have proper respect for the creatures sacrificed for our benefit.

I am more at home with that view because my childhood summers were rural. By the time I was seven or eight, I had done my share of fishing and hunting, and I'd been taught also to clean my catch or kill. I never shot anything larger than a pigeon or rabbit. That I was allowed to use a gun at all was the result of a remarkably indulgent father. He never took me deer hunting, not because I was a girl but because he couldn't bear to shoot them himself. But we ate venison brought to us by other men in the family.

I don't remember much being made of the sacredness of the life we took, but there was a real emphasis on fair play, much of it codified in law, like shooting game birds only on the wing, like not hunting deer with flashlights at night, like not shooting does. But my kinfold frowned on bait fishing as well. They were sportsmen who retained the wilderness ethic of not killing more than they could use. Strictly speaking, we did not need the food. (We could get meat in a town ten miles down the road.)But we did eat it.

Over the years, I became citified. I still could and did put live lobsters and crab in boiling water, but meat came from the meat market. Now that I live in the country again, I am much more aware of the slaughter that goes on around me, for I not only eat venison from the local hunt but have known the lamb and kid on the hoof (even in my rhododendrons, which is good for neither them nor the rhododendrons) which I eat. The killers of the animals are my moral, meat-eating neighbors. I have never killed a large animal, and I hope I never have to, though I'm not particularly tender-hearted about creatures not human. I find it hard to confront the struggle, smell, and mess of slaughter. I simply haven't the stomach for it. But, if I had to do it or go without meat, I would learn how.

It's puzzling to me that cannibalism is a fascinating abomination to vegetarian and meat eater alike, a habit claimed by only the most vicious and primitive tribes. We are scandalized by stories of the Donner Party or rumors of cannibalism at the site of a small plane crash in the wilderness, a boat lost at sea. Yet why would it be so horrifying for survivors to feed on the flesh of those who have died? Have worms and buzzards more right to the carcass?

We apparently do not think of ourselves as part of the food chain, except by cruel and exceptional accident. Our flesh, like the cow in India, is sacred and taboo, thought of as violated even when it is consigned to a mass grave. We bury it to hide a truth that still must be obvious to us, that as we eat so are we eaten. Why the lowly maggot is given the privilege (or sometimes the fish or the vulture) denied other living creatures is a complex puzzle of hygiene, myth and morality in each culture.

Our denial that we are part of nature, our sense of superiority to it, is our basic trouble. Though we are not, as the producers of margarine would make us believe, what we eat, we are related to what we harvest and kill. If being a vegetarian or a moral meat eater is a habit to remind us of that responsibility, neither is to be disrespected. When habit becomes a taboo, it blinds us to the real meaning. We are also related to each other, but our general refusal to eat our own flesh has not stopped us from slaughtering each other in large and totally wasted numbers.

I am flesh, a flesh eater, whether the food is carrot or cow. Harvesting and killing are the same activity, the interrupting of one life cycle for the sake of another. We don't stop at eating either. We kill to keep warm. We kill for shelter.

Back there in my rural childhood, I had not only a fishing rod and a rifle, I had a hatchet, too. I cleared brush, cut down small trees, chopped wood. I was present at the felling of a two-thousand-year-old redwood tree, whose impact shook the earth I stood on. It was a death more simply shocking to me than any other I've ever witnessed. The house I lived in then was made of redwood. The house I live in now is cedar.

My ashes may nourish the roots of a living tree, pitifully small compensation for the nearly immeasurable acres I have laid waste for my needs and pleasures, even for my work. For such omnivorous creatures as we are, a few frugal habits are not enough. We have to feed and midwife more than we slaughter, replant more than we harvest, if not with our hands, then with our own talents to see that it is done in our name, that we own to it.

The scallop shells will be finely cleaned by raccoons, then made by a neighbor into wind chimes, which may trouble my sleep and probably should until it is time for my own bones to sing.

A few of the publications of
THE NAIAD PRESS, INC.
P.O. Box 10543 • **Tallahassee, Florida 32302**
Mail orders welcome. Please include 15% postage.

A Hot-Eyed Moderate by Jane Rule. Essays. 252 pp.
    ISBN 0-930044-57-6 $7.95
    ISBN 0-930044-59-2 $13.95

Inland Passage and Other Stories by Jane Rule. 288 pp.
    ISBN 0-930044-56-8 $7.95
    ISBN 0-930044-58-4 $13.95

We Too Are Drifting by Gale Wilhelm. A novel. 128 pp.
    ISBN 0-930044-61-4 $6.95

Amateur City by Katherine V. Forrest. A mystery novel. 224 pp.
    ISBN 0-930044-55-X $7.95

The Sophie Horowitz Story by Sarah Schulman. A novel. 176 pp.
    ISBN 0-930044-54-1 $7.95

The Young in One Another's Arms by Jane Rule. A novel. 224 pp.
    ISBN 0-930044-53-3 $7.95

The Burnton Widows by Vicki P. McConnell. A mystery novel.
272 pp. ISBN 0-930044-52-5 $7.95

Old Dyke Tales by Lee Lynch. Short Stories. 224 pp.
    ISBN 0-930044-51-7 $7.95

Daughters of a Coral Dawn by Katherine V. Forrest. Science
fiction. 240 pp. ISBN 0-930044-50-9 $7.95

The Price of Salt by Claire Morgan. A novel. 288 pp.
    ISBN 0-930044-49-5 $7.95

Against the Season by Jane Rule. A novel. 224 pp.
    ISBN 0-930044-48-7 $7.95

Lovers in the Present Afternoon by Kathleen Fleming. A novel.
288 pp. ISBN 0-930044-46-0 $8.50

Toothpick House by Lee Lynch. A novel. 264 pp.
    ISBN 0-930044-45-2 $7.95

Madame Aurora by Sarah Aldridge. A novel. 256 pp.
    ISBN 0-930044-44-4 $7.95

Curious Wine by Katherine V. Forrest. A novel. 176 pp.
    ISBN 0-930044-43-6 $7.50

Black Lesbian in White America. Short stories, essays,
autobiography. 144 pp. ISBN 0-930044-41-X $7.50

Contract with the World by Jane Rule. A novel. 340 pp.
    ISBN 0-930044-28-2 $7.95

Yantras of Womanlove by Tee A. Corinne. Photographs.
64 pp. ISBN 0-930044-30-4 $6.95

Mrs. Porter's Letter by Vicki P. McConnell. A mystery novel.
224 pp. ISBN 0-930044-29-0 $6.95

To the Cleveland Station by Carol Anne Douglas. A novel.
192 pp. ISBN 0-930044-27-4 $6.95

The Nesting Place by Sarah Aldridge. A novel. 224 pp.
ISBN 0-930044-26-6 $6.95

This Is Not for You by Jane Rule. A novel. 284 pp.
ISBN 0-930044-25-8 $7.95

Faultline by Sheila Ortiz Taylor. A novel. 140 pp.
ISBN 0-930044-24-X $6.95

The Lesbian in Literature by Barbara Grier. 3d ed.
Foreword by Maida Tilchen. A comprehensive bibliography.
240 pp. ISBN 0-930044-23-1 $7.95

Anna's Country by Elizabeth Lang. A novel. 208 pp.
ISBN 0-930044-19-3 $6.95

Prism by Valerie Taylor. A novel. 158 pp.
ISBN 0-930044-18-5 $6.95

Black Lesbians: An Annotated Bibliography compiled by
JR Roberts. Foreword by Barbara Smith. 112 pp.
ISBN 0-930044-21-5 $5.95

The Marquise and the Novice by Victoria Ramstetter.
A novel. 108 pp. ISBN 0-930044-16-9 $4.95

Labiaflowers by Tee A. Corinne. 40 pp.
ISBN 0-930044-20-7 $3.95

Outlander by Jane Rule. Short stories, essays. 207 pp.
ISBN 0-930044-17-7 $6.95

Sapphistry: The Book of Lesbian Sexuality by Pat Califia.
2nd edition, revised. 195 pp. ISBN 0-930044-47-9 $7.95

The Black and White of It by Ann Allen Shockley.
Short stories. 112 pp. ISBN 0-930044-15-0 $5.95

All True Lovers by Sarah Aldridge. A novel. 292 pp.
ISBN 0-930044-10-X $6.95

A Woman Appeared to Me by Renee Vivien. Translated by
Jeannette H. Foster. A novel. xxxi, 65 pp.
ISBN 0-930044-06-1 $5.00

Cytherea's Breath by Sarah Aldridge. A novel. 240 pp.
ISBN 0-930044-02-9 $6.95

Tottie by Sarah Aldridge. A novel. 181 pp.
ISBN 0-930044-01-0 $6.95

The Latecomer by Sarah Aldridge. A novel. 107 pp.
ISBN 0-930044-00-2 $5.00

VOLUTE BOOKS

Journey to Fulfillment	by Valerie Taylor	$3.95
A World without Men	by Valerie Taylor	$3.95
Return to Lesbos	by Valerie Taylor	$3.95
Desert of the Heart	by Jane Rule	$3.95
Odd Girl Out	by Ann Bannon	$3.95
I Am a Woman	by Ann Bannon	$3.95
Women in the Shadows	by Ann Bannon	$3.95
Journey to a Woman	by Ann Bannon	$3.95
Beebo Brinker	by Ann Bannon	$3.95

These are just a few of the many Naiad Press titles. Please request a complete catalog!